"In My Office."

Pivoting on his heel, Max strode away down the hallway. He didn't look back to see if she was following. He expected obedience. He'd always been bossy that way. Telling her where to put her hands, how to move her hips, the areas of his body that enjoyed her attention.

Her skin flushed. Desire found a warm and welcoming home inside her. She couldn't move. What was she doing? Her memories of those four days with Max belonged in the tomb with all her girlish hopes and dreams. Indulging in lusty thoughts of Max was the height of stupidity if she hoped to cultivate a professional relationship with him.

Max disappeared around a corner. This was her chance to run. She'd been a fool to think she could ever put those magical days behind her. She should make some excuse.

No. Rachel squared her shoulders. She could do this. She had to do this. Her future required it.

Dear Reader,

When I found out Harlequin Books wanted to publish *Meddling with a Millionaire,* I was consumed with the idea of writing books about all three Case brothers. I have always been a fan of connected stories, and from the number of readers asking for Max's story, I realized I wasn't alone.

Although *Unfinished Business* is the third Case brother story, it was actually the second one I wrote. Max was so clear in my mind because he has such a hard time letting go of past wrongs. For me, he was the most frustrating of the three brothers. So naturally he was the most fun to write.

A stubborn man deserves a strong woman, and that's what Max gets in Rachel Lansing. Misguided decisions in her past have created a woman who refuses to let anyone help her. And with everything going on in her life, Rachel can use some help.

Reunion stories are my favorite. Take two people who are passionate about each other, toss in something that tears them apart, let their anger stew for a few years and then serve up a situation that forces them to work together. Sounds like the perfect recipe for romance to me.

I hope you enjoy Max and Rachel's story.

Happy reading.

Cat Schield

www.catschield.com

CAT SCHIELD

UNFINISHED BUSINESS

Harlequin®

Desire

Recycling programs
for this product may
not exist in your area.

ISBN-13: 978-0-373-73166-4

UNFINISHED BUSINESS

www.Harlequin.com

Printed in U.S.A.

Books by Cat Schield

Harlequin Desire

Meddling with a Millionaire #2094
A Win-Win Proposition #2116
Unfinished Business #2153

Other titles by this author available in ebook format.

CAT SCHIELD

has been reading and writing romance since high school. Although she graduated from college with a B.A. in business, her idea of a perfect career was writing for Harlequin Books. And now, after winning the Romance Writers of America 2010 Golden Heart Award for series contemporary romance, that dream has come true. Cat lives in Minnesota with her daughter, Emily, and their Burmese cat. When she's not writing sexy, romantic stories for Harlequin Desire, she can be found sailing with friends on the St. Croix River or in more exotic locales like the Caribbean and Europe. She loves to hear from readers. Find her at www.catschield.com. Follow her on Twitter @catschield.

For my parents.
Your love and support have helped me follow my dreams.

One

"You." The word came out as an unfriendly accusation.

"Hello, Max."

Rachel Lansing had been bracing herself for this meeting all day, and now that it had arrived, it was so much worse than she'd imagined. Her heart stopped as the gunmetal gray of Max Case's gaze slammed into her with all the delicacy of a sledgehammer.

She dug her fingernails into her palm as his broad shoulders loomed closer, blocking her view of the tastefully decorated lobby with its soothing navy-and-olive walls and stunning original art.

Was it her imagination or did Max seem bigger, more commanding than the creative lover that haunted her memories? Or maybe his presence overwhelmed her because in a charcoal business suit and silver tie, he was less approachable than the naked fantasy man that frequented her dreams.

Only the public nature of this reunion enabled her to

subdue the flight impulse in her muscles. She rose from the comfortable couch in the reception area at a deliberate, unhurried pace. Keeping her body relaxed and her expression professional required a Herculean effort while her pulse jittered and her knees shook.

Pull yourself together. He won't appreciate you melting into a puddle at his feet.

"Thank you for seeing me." She stuck out her hand in a bid to restore her professional standing and wasn't disappointed when Max ignored it. Her sweaty palm would betray her nerves to him.

When he remained mute, Rachel plowed into the tense silence. "How great that Andrea had her baby. And two weeks early. Sabrina told me she had a boy. I brought her this." She raised her left hand to show him the pink and blue bag dangling from her fingers. She'd bought the gift for his assistant weeks ago and was disappointed she wouldn't get to see Andrea's expression when she opened it.

"What are you doing here?"

"I was supposed to meet with Andrea."

"You're with the employment agency?"

She whipped out a business card and extended it across the three feet that separated them. "I own it." She made no attempt to disguise her pride at what she'd accomplished.

He rubbed his thumb over the lettering on the business card before glancing down. "Rachel...Lansing?"

"My maiden name." She wasn't sure why she felt compelled to share this tidbit with him. It wasn't going to change how he felt about her now, was it?

"You're divorced?"

She nodded. "Four years."

"And now you run an employment agency here in Houston?"

She'd come a long way from the girl who was barely able

to support herself and her sister on the tips she made wait-ressing in a beach restaurant in Gulf Shores, Alabama. And yet, how far had she come when no matter how well her busi-ness did, she never felt financially secure?

"I like the freedom of running my own business," she said, pushing aside the worry that drove her day and night. "It's small, but growing."

And it would grow faster once she moved into larger of-fices and hired more staff. She had the space all picked out. A prime location that wouldn't have lasted on the market more than a few days. She'd signed the lease yesterday, gambling that the commission she'd get from placing a temporary as-sistant with Case Consolidated Holdings would give her the final amount she needed to move. Maybe then she could stop living day to day and start planning for the future. However, now that she'd run into Max, that fee seemed in jeopardy, and just to be safe, she'd better back out of the lease.

If only Devon had been able to come here in her stead. A skilled employment specialist, he was her right hand. Unfor-tunately, his mother had gone to the hospital yesterday with severe abdominal pain and had been rushed into surgery to remove her gall bladder. Rachel had told Devon to stay with his mother as long as she needed him. For Rachel, family always came first.

"How many assistants have you placed here?" Max's pierc-ing stare didn't waver from her face as he slid her business card into his breast pocket. The effect of so much icy heat coming to bear on her was starting to unravel her composure.

"Five." She dropped her hand into her jacket pocket to keep from plucking at her collar, lapel or buttons and betray-ing her disquiet. "Missy was the first. Sebastian's assistant."

"That was your doing?"

Rachel blinked at the soft menace in his voice. Did Max have something against Missy? She'd been with Case Consolidated Holdings for four years and had worked out great. In fact, it was that placement that had jump-started her business.

"I heard she recently got promoted to communications director." And married Max's brother, Sebastian. Surely that proved how good Rachel was at her job.

"That means you've been in Houston four years?" The question rumbled out of Max like a guard-dog growl.

Anxiety spiked. "About that."

"Why here?"

When she'd left him in the Alabama beach town, he'd never wanted to see her again. Was he wondering if it was fate or determined stalking on her part that she'd shown up at Case Consolidated Holdings?

"I moved here because of my sister. She went to the University of Houston and has friends here. It made sense for us to settle in Houston after she graduated."

Inferring that Rachel hadn't had friends where she'd lived before. Curiosity fired in Max's eyes. The intensity of it seared her nerve endings. Five years had passed since she'd last seen him and her physical response to his proximity hadn't dimmed one bit.

"I have three clients in this building," she told him, her tone firming as she reclaimed her confidence. She'd been dealing with executives for over ten years and knew exactly how to handle them. "The fact that I've placed five assistants here and we've never run across each other should tell you that my interest in your company is purely professional."

He surveyed her like a cop in search of the truth. "Let's talk."

"I thought that's what we were doing." She bit the inside of her lip as the smart-ass remark popped out.

Once upon a time he'd liked her cheeky banter. She doubted he'd say the same thing today. Five years was a long time to stay mad at someone, but if anyone could manage, it would be Max Case.

"In my office."

Pivoting on his heel, he strode away from her down the hallway that led into the bowels of Case Consolidated Holdings. He didn't look back to see if she was following. He expected obedience. He'd always been bossy that way. Telling her where to put her hands, how to move her hips, the areas of his body that needed her attention.

Her skin flushed. Desire found a warm and welcoming home inside her. She couldn't move. What was she doing? Her memories of those four days with Max belonged in the tomb with all her girlish hopes and dreams. Her moratorium on men and sex remained in full force. Indulging in lusty thoughts of Max was the height of stupidity if she hoped to cultivate a professional relationship with him.

Max disappeared around a corner. This was her chance to run. She should make some excuse. Send Devon to do the interview tomorrow.

No. Rachel squared her shoulders. She could do this. She had to do this. Her future required this placement fee.

Five years ago, she'd learned a hard lesson about running from her problems. These days, she faced all difficulties head-on. Lansing Employment Agency needed this commission. She would do a fabulous job for Max, collect her money and treat herself to a bottle of champagne and a long bubble bath the day the agency moved into its bigger, better office. It all started with this meeting.

Rachel forced her feet to move. Step by step she gathered courage. For four years she'd been scraping and clawing her way upward. Convincing Max that Lansing was the agency for him was just one more hurdle, and by the time she reached the enormous office bearing Max's name, she had her chin set at a determined angle and her eyes focused on the prize.

"Did you get lost?" he asked as she crossed the threshold.

A long time ago.

"I stopped at Sabrina's desk and asked her to send the baby gift to Andrea."

Rachel glanced around Max's office, curious about the businessman. During their four days together, she'd learned about his family and his love of fast cars, but he'd refused to talk about work. In fact, until she'd met Sebastian four years ago, and noticed the family resemblance, she didn't know he was Max Case of Case Consolidated Holdings.

The walls bore photos of Max leaning against a series of racecars, helmet beneath his arm, a confident grin on his face. Her heart jumped in appreciation of how handsome he looked in his one-piece navy-and-gray racing suit, lean hips and broad shoulders emphasized by the stylish cut. A bookshelf held a few trophies, and books on muscle cars.

"You cut your hair." Max shut the door, blocking her escape.

She searched his expression, but he'd shut all emotion behind an impassive mask. His eyes were the blank stone walls of a fortress. Nevertheless, his personal comment aroused a tickle of awareness.

"Never liked it long." Her ex-husband had, however.

A softening of his lips looked suspiciously like the beginnings of a smile. Did he recognize her attempt to camouflage herself? Shapeless gray pantsuit, short hair, no jewelry of any kind, a sensible watch, flat shoes, minimal makeup. Dull as dirt to look at, but confident and authoritative about her business. She'd never been any man's fantasy. Too tall for most boys. Too flat-chested and skinny for the rest, the best she'd been able to hope for from her male classmates in high school was best friend or buddy. She'd grown up playing soccer, basketball and baseball with the guys.

Which is why it continued to blow her mind that a man

like Maxwell Case, who could have any woman he wanted, had wanted her once upon a time.

An enormous cherry desk dominated a position in front of the windows. The piece seemed too clunky for Max. Rachel pictured him behind an aerodynamic glass and chrome desk loaded down with the latest computer gadgets.

Instead of leading the way toward his desk, Max settled on the couch that occupied one wall of his office. With a flick of his hand, he indicated a flanking chair. Disliking the informality of the setting, Rachel perched on the very edge of the seat. Her briefcase on her lap acted as both a shield and a reminder that this was a business meeting.

"I need an executive assistant here first thing tomorrow."

Rachel hadn't been prepared for Andrea to have her baby two weeks early. She had no one available that was skilled enough to fill in starting in the morning. "I have the perfect person for you, but she can't start until Monday."

"That won't do."

With her commission slipping away, panic crept into her voice. "It's only two days. Surely you can make it without an assistant until Monday."

"With Andrea gone today, I'm already behind. We're up to our necks in next year's budgets. I need someone who can get up to speed swiftly. Someone with world-class organizational skills." His focus sharpened on her. "Someone like you. You're exactly what I need."

Her gut clenched at the flare of something white hot in his eyes.

A matching blaze roared to life inside her. Five years ago, that similar fire had charred her self-protective instincts and reduced her sensible nature to ash. She'd flung herself headlong into his arms without considering the repercussions.

The last time she'd lost herself that way, he'd ended up hating her. Meeting his gaze, she realized that his anger hadn't been blunted by the passing years. Time hadn't healed. It had honed his resentment into a razor-sharp tool for revenge.

Rachel braced herself against the earthquake of panic that threatened her peaceful little world and set her jaw. "You can't have me."

Her declaration hung in the air.

But he could have her...

As his assistant.

In any of the dozens of ways he'd had her before.

His choice. Not hers.

Energy zipped between them, fascinating and unsettling. The scent of her perfume aroused memories. Reminded him how sharp and sweet the desire was between them.

"Are you really ready to risk disappointing a client?"

"No." A rosy flush dusted her high cheekbones. Had she picked up on his thoughts? "But I can't abandon my business to be your assistant."

"Hire someone to fill in for you." He bared his teeth in an unfriendly grin. "Even you can see the irony in that."

For the last few minutes, cracks had been developing in her professionalism. "You're being unreasonable."

"Of course I am. I'll call someone else." The telltale widening of her eyes was gone so fast he nearly missed it. This is where he challenged her reputation for providing excellent customer service to test how badly she wanted his business. "I'm sure another agency would have what I need."

"Lansing Employment has what you need," she countered, the words muddy because she spoke through clenched teeth.

He held silent while she tried to stare him down. Every instinct told him to send her on her way as he would any other supplier who couldn't provide him with exactly what he wanted.

But they had unfinished business. At some point in the last five minutes he'd decided he needed closure. Four days with her hadn't been enough time for the passion to burn out. Much to his dismay, he still wanted her. But for how long was anyone's guess. From past experience he knew his interest rarely lasted more than two months.

And when he grew tired of her, he would end things on his terms. On his schedule.

"Fine." She glared at him. "I'll fill in for two days."

"Wonderful."

She stood, ready to stalk out of the office, but something held her in place. Her eyes were troubled as they settled on him. "Why are you doing this?"

"Doing what?"

"Demanding that I act as your assistant until I can find a replacement."

"You're here. It's expedient."

His current workload was crushing him. His managers had finalized their forecasts and forwarded next year's budget numbers a week ago. With the economy slow to recover, controlling spending and increasing sales was more important than ever. Case Consolidated Holdings owned over a dozen companies, each one with very different markets and operations. It was an organizational challenge to collect and analyze data from the various sources given that each entity operated in a completely unique environment with it's own set of parameters and strategic plans.

Andrea knew the businesses as well as he did. Losing her now threw off his entire schedule.

"Are you sure that's all it is?" Rachel demanded.

Max stopped worrying about deadlines and reminded himself that his desperate staffing situation was only half the reason he'd insisted Rachel fill in for a few days. "What else could it be?"

"Payback for how things ended between us?"

"It's business." That she was suspicious of his motives added spice to the game.

"So, you're not still angry?" she persisted.

Yes. He was still angry.

"After five years?" He shook his head.

"Are you sure?"

"Are you challenging whether or not I know my own mind?"

His irritation had little effect on her. "Five years ago, you made it very clear you never wanted to see me again."

"That's because you never told me you were married." He kept his tone smooth, but it wasn't enough to mask his dangerous mood. "Despite my telling you how I felt about infidelity. How it nearly destroyed my parents' marriage. You involved me in an extramarital affair without my knowledge."

"I'd left my husband."

He breathed deep to ease the sudden ache in his chest. "Yet when he showed up, you went back to him fast enough."

"Things were complicated."

"I didn't see complications. I saw lies."

"I was going through some tough times. Meeting you let me forget my troubles for a while."

"You used me."

She tipped her head and regarded him through her long lashes. "We used each other."

Max's gaze roamed over her. She wasn't the most beautiful woman he'd ever met. Her nose was too narrow. Her chin a bit too sharp. She hid her broad forehead with bangs. Boyishly slim, her body lacked the feminine curves he usually appreciated in a woman. But there was something lush about the fullness of her lips. And he'd adored nibbling his way down her long, graceful neck.

He wasn't surprised to be struck by a blast of lust so intense, it hurt. From the first, the chemistry between them had been hot and all consuming. The instant he recognized her in the lobby, he knew that hadn't changed.

For a second, doubts crept in. Would spending time with her open old wounds? The last time they'd parted, he'd been out of sorts for months. Of course, he'd been in a different place then. Full of optimism about love and marriage despite the painful lessons about infidelity he'd learned from his father's actions.

Thanks to Rachel, his heart was no longer open for business.

"What time should I be here tomorrow morning?"

"Eight."

She headed for the door and he let his gaze slide over her utilitarian gray suit. One word kept rolling over and over in his mind. Divorced.

Fair game.

She hesitated in the doorway, her back to him, face in profile. Her quiet, determined voice floated toward him over her shoulder. "Two days. No more."

Without a backward glance, she vanished from view. Sexy as hell. She'd always had an aura of the untouchable about her. As if no matter how many times he slid inside her, or how tight he wrapped her in his arms, she would never truly be his.

For a man accustomed to having any woman he wanted, that elusive quality intrigued him the way nothing else would have. He couldn't get enough of her. They'd been together for four days. He'd been insatiable. But no matter how much pleasure he gave her, no matter how many times she came apart in his arms, not once did he come close to capturing her soul.

It wasn't until she left him and went back to her husband that he'd understood why.

Her soul wasn't hers to give. It belonged to the man she'd pledged her life and love to.

Rage catapulted Max from his chair. He crossed to his door and slammed it shut, not caring what the office thought of his fit of temper. His hand shook as he braced it against the wall.

Damn her for showing up like this.

And damn the part of him that was delighted she had.

Two

Rachel hurried through the plate glass doors of Lansing Employment Agency and nodded to her receptionist as she passed. She didn't stop to chat as was her habit, but went straight to her office and collapsed into her chair. It wasn't until she'd deleted half her inbox that she realized she hadn't read any of the emails. Sagging forward, she rested her arms on the desk and her forehead on her arms. Reaction was setting in. She was frustratingly close to tears.

"That bad, huh?" a male voice asked from the hallway.

Rachel nodded without looking up. "It's worse than bad."

"Oh, you poor thing. Tell Devon all about it."

With a great effort, Rachel straightened and looked at the man who sat down across from her. In a stylish gray suit with lavender shirt and expensive purple tie, he dressed to be noticed. Only the dark circles beneath his eyes gave any hint of his sleepless night.

"How's your mother?"

"She's doing fine. My sister just arrived from Austin and is staying at the hospital with her." Devon leaned back in his chair and crossed one leg over the other. "How'd it go at Case Consolidated Holdings?"

"Worse than I'd hoped."

"Damn. They didn't hire us?"

"They hired us." Rachel's eyes burned dry and hot. As she blinked to restore moisture, it occurred to her that she'd cried a river of tears over Max five years ago. Maybe she'd used up her quota.

"Then what's the problem?"

"Max Case needs an assistant immediately."

"But we don't have anyone available."

Rachel grimaced. "That's why I'm filling in until we do."

"You?" The gap between Devon's front teeth flashed as a startled laugh escaped him.

No one knew what had happened between her and Max in Gulf Shores. She figured if she kept it to herself, no one could criticize her for running away from her farce of a marriage and jumping into bed with a virtual stranger, and those amazing four days could remain untarnished in her memory. But she'd been wrong to start something with Max before she'd legally ended her marriage. And she'd paid the price.

"I was the expedient choice." The word tasted bitter on her tongue. Why had it bothered her that she was merely a convenient business solution to Max? Had she really hoped he might still want her after she'd kept quiet about her marital status, and let him betray his vow never to get caught up in an affair?

Those days in Max's arms had been magical. She hadn't felt that safe since her father died. It was as if she and Max existed in a bubble of perfect happiness. Insulated from the world's harsh reality.

Heaven.

Until Brody showed up with his threats and dragged her back to Mississippi.

"I hope you told him no."

"Not exactly."

"Then what exactly?" Her second in command frowned as if just now grasping the situation.

"It's not like he left me any choice. I signed the lease for the new offices. We need this placement fee to move into them."

"You agreed?"

"He backed me against a wall." She leaned back in her chair, remembering too late that the ancient mechanism was broken. She threw her weight forward before the cursed thing tipped her ass over teakettle.

Devon oversaw her antics with troubled eyes. "I still don't understand why he wants you personally. There are a dozen agencies that he could call."

She hesitated. As much as she liked Devon, she wasn't comfortable talking about her past. Five years ago, she'd been a very different person. Explaining how she knew Max meant she had to own up to the mistakes she'd made. Mistakes that haunted her.

"Once upon a time we knew each other," she said.

"Knew…" Devon's focus sharpened. "As in business associates? Friends?" His eyes narrowed. "You dated?"

As much as she hated talking about her past screwups, she decided to put her cards on the table. She owed Devon the truth. He'd been with her since the beginning and had labored as hard as she had to grow the agency. In fact, she was planning on making him a partner when they moved into the new offices.

If they moved.

"Not dated, exactly." She played with her pen, spinning it in circles on her desk.

"You slept with him."

"Yes."

Rachel shifted her attention from the silver blur and caught Devon's stunned expression. He looked so thunderstruck she was torn between laughter and outrage.

"Don't look so surprised. I wasn't always the uptight businesswoman I am now. There was a time when I was young and romantic." And foolish.

"When?"

"A long weekend five years ago."

Devon's lips twitched.

"What?" she demanded.

"It's just that Max is well-known for the volume of women he dates. I'm a little surprised he remembered you."

"He probably wouldn't have," she muttered. The truth hit closer to her insecurities than she wanted to admit. The thought had often crossed her mind that she'd had a pretty brief interlude with Max. Since moving to Houston, she'd learned a lot about the man who'd swept her off her feet in a big way. She'd often wondered how she'd feel if she ran into him and he looked right through her without recognition. "Except he was pretty angry with me at the time."

"Why?"

"Because I didn't tell him I was married."

Now Devon really goggled at her. "We've worked together four years and this is the first I've heard about that."

Rachel rubbed her right thumb across the ring finger of her left hand. Even after four years, she recalled the touch of the gold band against her skin and remembered how wrong she'd been to ignore her instincts. She wouldn't make that mistake again.

"It's part of my past that I'd prefer not to talk about." And in five more years, she'd be completely free. At least financially. She'd live with the emotional scars for the rest of her life.

"Not even if I tell you I'll expire from curiosity if you don't dish?"

"Not even," Rachel said with a chuckle. She loved Devon's flare for the dramatic. Having him around was good for her. Kept her from taking herself, or her problems, too seriously. She'd done that all too often in the past and turned molehills into mountains.

"Do you think Max is trying to start up with you again?"

From one unwelcome topic to another. "Hardly."

"I don't know." Devon shot her an odd look, half surprised, half crafty. "Demanding you act as his assistant, even for a couple days, seems a little odd for a businessman with Max's no-nonsense reputation."

Rachel exhaled. "Well, there's not much I can do at the moment. He's set on having me there." She grimaced. "Besides, you'll do great without me. Lansing Employment Agency wouldn't be anywhere near profitable without all your hard work."

"Yes, yes, I'm wonderful but the success has been all yours. I've just been along for the ride."

And what a ride it had been. When she'd first started the agency, she'd been waitressing on the weekends to make rent and put food on the table.

Today, providing things went right with Case Consolidated Holdings, they'd be moving into larger downtown Houston offices. That's why she was willing to do whatever Max wanted of her to stay on his good side.

"I just hope you know what you're doing," Devon said, getting to his feet.

"I know exactly what I'm doing." Her stomach gave a funny little flip as she said the words. Rachel shoved the sensation away. She was a professional. She would not allow her emotions to get all tangled up in Max again. The first time had left her with a battered heart. Letting it happen again might lead to serious breakage.

"You're a first-rate bastard, you know that?"

Max Case looked away from the photo on his computer screen and smirked at his best friend. "I've been called that before."

It was late Friday morning. He'd spent the last day and a half alternating between admiration for Rachel's keen business mind and annoyance that he couldn't stop imagining her writhing beneath him on his couch.

"I've been after Sikes to sell me that car for five years," Jason Sinclair grumbled, his gaze riveted on the image of Max standing beside a yellow convertible. "And you just swoop in and steal it out from under me?"

"I didn't swoop, and I didn't steal. I offered the guy a good price. He went for it."

"How much?"

Max shook his head. He wasn't about to tell Jason the truth. In fact, he wasn't exactly sure what had prompted him to offer the sum. He only knew that Bob Sikes had driven the rare muscle car off the lot in 1971 and wasn't about to let it go without some major convincing. The Cuda 426 Hemi convertible was one of only seven made. At the time, convertibles were too expensive, too heavy and too slow to interest the true racing enthusiasts. Thus, with fewer produced, they'd become extremely rare.

And now, Max owned one of the rarest of the rare.

"Are you ready to get your ass kicked in tomorrow's race?" He meant for the question to distract his friend.

"You sound awfully confident for a man who lost last weekend." Jason continued to frown over the loss of the Cuda. "A win that put me ahead of you in points."

"For now."

Max and Jason had been racing competitively since they were old enough to drive. They were evenly matched in determination, skill, and financing, so on any given weekend, the win could go either way.

For the last two years, Max had beaten Jason in points over the course of the season. Like the street racers of old, Jason and Max competed for cars. The guy with fewer points at the end of the season forfeited his ride. But Max knew coming in second bothered his best friend more than the forfeit of his racecar two years straight.

Jason adopted a confident pose. "If you think you're going to have the most points again this year, you're wrong."

Before Max could answer, Rachel appeared in his office doorway. Despite her severe navy pantsuit and plain white blouse, his pulse behaved as if she wore a provocative cocktail dress and a come-hither smile.

"Excuse me, Max. I didn't realize you had company."

He waved Rachel in. "Did you get those numbers I needed?"

She took one step into the room and stopped. "I updated the report." She glanced in Jason's direction. "I also scheduled an interview for you at two this afternoon and emailed you the candidate's resume. Maureen has a background in finance and business analysis. I think you'll find she's a perfect fit."

"We'll see."

Her lips thinned. "Yes, you will."

Amusement rippled through him as she tossed her head and exited his office. Did she have any idea that annoyance gave her stride a sexy swing?

"Hell."

Max noticed Jason was also staring after Rachel. "What?"

"That was Rachel Lansing. What is she doing here?"

"Working as my assistant."

"Have you lost your mind?"

Probably. But Jason didn't know about his affair with Rachel. No one did. Those four days had been too short and too intense. The end too painful for him to share. And after badmouthing his father's infidelity for years, how could he admit to family and friends that he'd had an affair with a married woman and not be viewed as a hypocrite?

"What are you talking about?"

"Lansing is a matchmaker."

"A what?" Max searched his best friend's serious expression for some sign that Jason was joking around.

"Lansing Employment Agency is a matchmaking service."

"You're kidding, right?" He was deeply concerned that his friend might not be.

Jason glared at him. "Don't look at me like that. You have no idea what you're dealing with."

Rubbing his eyes, Max sighed. "Right now I'm dealing with a lunatic." Confusion and amusement jockeyed for dominance. He'd never seen his best friend exhibit such over-the-top behavior.

"It's not funny."

A gust of laughter escaped him. "Sit in my chair for a minute, and I think you'll see it's really funny."

"My dad used Lansing last year." Jason's eyebrows arched. "He married his executive assistant six months later."

"Your dad was a widower for fifteen years. I'm a little surprised he didn't remarry a lot sooner. Besides, Claire is a knockout."

"You're missing the point. They're all knockouts."

"So," Max drawled. "It's a conspiracy?"

"Yes." The thirty-two-year-old CFO stopped looking wild-eyed and his attention settled laser-sharp on Max. Jason's chest lifted as he pulled in an enormous breath. "You think I'm crazy?"

"Certifiable."

"I know of five other guys that have hired their assistants from Lansing and ended up marrying them. I know two more guys that met their future wives at work. Wives that got their jobs thanks to the Lansing Employment Agency. Including your brother." Jason's lips thinned. "Still think I'm nuts?"

"How did you find all this out?"

Jason shrugged. "Do you really need to ask? After Dad started looking all gooey-eyed at Claire, I did a little research on the agency."

"What did you find?"

"A spotless reputation. And one hell of a track record."

"For what?"

"For turning executive assistants into wives."

"Don't you think that eight marriages out of hundreds of placements is a little insignificant?"

"It's more worrisome when you take into consideration the ratio of single executives with single assistants to married executives with married assistants."

"You lost me."

"The bulk of the executives are already married, so when you look at the numbers in that way…"

"The ratio looks worse."

Jason flung his hands forward in a that's-what-I'm-talking-about gesture, before sinking back with a relieved smile. "Exactly."

Max was still having a hard time swallowing the notion of Rachel as a matchmaker. "Well, you don't need to worry about me. Where Cupid's arrows are concerned, I'm wearing Kevlar."

Jason pointed a finger at him. "You can't be sure of that."

"On the contrary, I'm very sure."

"I'm not really feeling convinced," the CFO said. "Maybe you'd care to make things more interesting."

Max buzzed with the same adrenaline that filled him at the start of every race. "What'd you have in mind?"

"Your '71 Cuda."

"Double my punishment, double your fun?" Max snorted. "I lose my freedom and the rarest car in my collection?" Suddenly, he wasn't feeling much like laughing. "What sort of best friend are you?"

"The kind that has your best interests at heart. I figure you might not fight to stay single for the sake of your sanity, but you'll do whatever it takes to keep that car."

Interesting logic. Max couldn't fault Jason's reasoning. "And what are you putting on the table in case you lose?"

Now it was Jason's turn to frown. "You want my '69 Corvette?" He shook his head. "I just got it."

And Max was looking forward to taking it away. "What are you worried about?"

"Fine. You've got a deal." Jason got to his feet and extended his hand across Max's wide cherry desk. When you've met the girl of your dreams and gotten married, I'm going to miss you, buddy. But at least I'll have the '71 Cuda to remember you by."

Rachel sat at her desk outside Max's office and tried to concentrate as her nerves sang a chorus of warnings. For the last two days, he'd been professional, making no further references to their past. But his gaze on her at odd moments held a particular intensity that promised he wasn't done with her. Not by a long shot.

Despite his assurances otherwise, she suspected that his motives for strong-arming her into becoming his temporary assistant were personal. She wouldn't put it past him to lure her into bed, enjoy his fill, and then walk away in the same fashion he believed she'd walked away from him. And that wasn't her paranoia talking. Max wasn't someone who forgave easily or at all in the case of his youngest brother, Nathan, and their father.

From what she'd gathered from her sources inside Case Consolidated Holdings, ever since Nathan had blown into town almost a year earlier, tension amongst the Case brothers had risen. She'd learned from Max five years ago that there was bad blood between the older Case brothers and their illegitimate brother that went way back. According to Andrea, however, things had recently gotten better between Sebastian and Nathan.

If Max couldn't let go of the past where his family was concerned, he would certainly never forgive a woman he barely knew.

Shoving personal concerns aside, Rachel concentrated on something she could control. Max had a trip scheduled next week. The hotel arrangements and flight had been made some time ago, but she needed to arrange for a rental car, to work on a PowerPoint presentation and fix a hundred problems that hadn't even come up yet.

The phone rang. Anxiety gripped her at the familiar number lighting up the screen. "Tell me everything's running smoothly," she said into the receiver.

"You sound edgy." Devon's amusement came through loud and clear. "Is Max on your case?"

While Devon laughed at his joke, Rachel signed on to the computer using Andrea's ID and password. At the moment, Max was interviewing a candidate for his temporary executive assistant. If all went well, Rachel wouldn't need to contact the IT department for her own computer access. She scanned the assistant's contacts, searching for the phone number of the restaurant downstairs. Apparently, Max had his lunches catered in most days. Andrea's contacts gave Rachel a pretty good sense of Max's activities.

Restaurants. Florists. Even a couple jewelry stores. He enjoyed entertaining women. Clicking one particular restaurant Rachel had been dying to try except that it was way beyond her means, she saw the manager's name, the particular table Max preferred, even the wine he enjoyed.

The man was a player. She hadn't seen that about him during those days on the beach, although she'd figured it out since coming to Houston. Max didn't know it, but she'd seen him in action during her early days in the big city.

Rachel stretched a barricade of caution tape around her heart. If Max wanted to start something with her with the express purpose of payback, she'd better be wary.

"...doing?"

Devon had been talking the whole time her mind had been wandering. Whoops.

"I'm sorry, Devon. I wasn't listening. What did you ask?"

"How is it going with Maureen?"

"She just went in ten minutes ago. Max kept her waiting for half an hour."

"I know that tone. Stop worrying. She's perfect. Max won't find anything wrong with her skills or her references."

"I hope not."

And she didn't have long to wait to find out. Five minutes after she'd hung up with Devon, Maureen exited Max's office. Unsure whether to be delighted or concerned at the shortness of the interview, Rachel stood as the assistant candidate headed her way.

"How'd it go?"

The beautiful redhead's mouth drooped. "He didn't seem to like me."

"Max is very hard to read. I'm sure he found your qualifications and your experience exactly what he requested."

Rachel kept her expression cheery. "I'll go have a chat with him now and give you a call later."

"Thanks."

As soon as Maureen disappeared around the corner, Rachel headed into Max's office. "Isn't Maureen great? She has a BA in business and five years of experience in a brokerage house. She's great with numbers—"

"Not a self-starter."

How had he come to that conclusion after a fifteen-minute interview? "That's not what I heard from her references."

"She's not going to work out. I need someone who takes initiative. Find me someone else."

Rachel hid her clenched hands behind her back and concentrated on keeping her shoulders relaxed and tension from her face as her mind worked furiously on an alternative candidate. "I'll set up someone for you to interview on Monday."

"Single?"

His question came out of left field and caught her completely off guard. "By law we don't discuss anyone's marital status."

"But they'd be wearing wedding rings. You'd know if they were single or married."

"I could guess…" She floundered. What did he want? Someone single he could hit on? That didn't seem right. Max might be a player, but he wouldn't be unprofessional at work. Seeing he awaited the answer to his earlier question, she heaved a sigh. "She's single. Does that matter?"

"Your agency has a certain reputation." He didn't make that sound like a compliment.

"For providing the best."

"For matchmaking."

Rachel wasn't sure if she'd heard him right. "Matchmaking? Are you out of your mind?" The words erupted before she considered how they might sound. Taking a calming breath, she moderated her tone. "I run an employment agency."

He nodded. "And how many of your clients have married the assistants you've sent them?"

What the hell sort of question was that? "I don't know."

"Eight, including Sebastian and Missy."

Rachel didn't know what to make of his accusation. Is that why he sounded so annoyed earlier? He thought… She didn't quite know what he thought. A matchmaking service? Was he insane?

"Don't look so surprised," he muttered.

"But I am. How did you know that?"

"A friend of mine has done a fair amount of research on your little enterprise." He sneered the last word, leaving no doubt about his opinion of her or her company.

Rachel inched forward on the sofa as she wavered between staying and disputing his claims and walking out the door. Fortunately, her business sense kicked in and kept her from acting impulsively.

"I assure you I'm not in the business of matchmaking." She straightened her spine and leveled a hard look at him. "My agency is strictly professional. If my ability to find the perfect match between executive and assistant means that they're compatible in other ways, then that's coincidence." Serendipity. She grimaced. If word got out that something unprofessional was happening between her clients and her employees, she was finished. "If you're worried about finding yourself in a similar predicament, I'll only send you married assistants."

She recognized her mistake the second the words were out of her mouth. Annoyance tightened his lips and hardened his eyes to tempered steel.

Once upon a time she'd been married, and he'd fallen for her. Well, maybe fallen for her was pushing it a little. They'd enjoyed a spectacular four days together and he'd been interested in pursuing her beyond the weekend.

"Or really old and ugly assistants," she finished lamely.

One eyebrow twitched upward to meet the lock of wavy brown hair that had fallen onto his forehead.

Rachel's professionalism came close to crumpling beneath the weight of his enormous sex appeal. Fortunately, the grim set of his mouth reminded her that they hadn't parted on the best of terms. He wouldn't appreciate the feminine sigh bottled up in her chest.

"I'll arrange some candidates for you to interview on Monday," she said, her heart sinking as she realized she was now stuck acting as Max's assistant for the indefinite future.

Three

Monday came and went and Max was no closer to liking any of the candidates she'd arranged for him to interview. By the time Rachel pulled into her driveway at six-thirty, she was half-starved and looking forward to her sister's famous chili. It was Hailey's night to cook, thank heavens, or they'd be eating around midnight.

She entered the house through the kitchen door and sniffed the air in search of the spicy odors that signaled Rachel was going to need three glasses of milk to get through the meal. No pot bubbled on the stove. No jalapeño cornbread cooled on a rack. Rachel's stomach growled in disappointment. No pile of dirty dishes awaited her attention in the sink. Why hadn't Hailey started dinner?

"I'm home," she called, stripping off her suit coat and setting her briefcase just inside the door. "I'm sorry I'm late. The new boss is a workaholic. Did you…"

Her question trailed away as she entered her small living

room and spied her sister's tense expression. Hailey perched on the edge of their dad's old recliner, her palms together and tucked between her knees. The chair was the only piece of furniture they'd kept after he died. That and the family's single photo album were all the Lansing girls had left of their dad.

Hailey's gaze darted Rachel's way as she paused just inside the room. Rachel's stomach gave a sickening wrench at the misery her sister couldn't hide. Only one person in the world produced the particular combination of alarm and disgust pinching Hailey's lips together.

Rachel turned her attention from her sister's stricken gaze to the tall man who dominated her couch. He'd grown fleshy in the four years since she'd last seen him, his boyish good looks warped by overindulgence and the belief that the world owed him something. He still dressed like the son of a wealthy and powerful business owner. Charcoal slacks, a white polo, blue sweater draped over his shoulders. He looked harmless until you got close enough to see the malicious glee in his eye.

"What are you doing here?"

He smiled without warmth. "Is that any way to greet the man you swore to honor and cherish until death you do part?" His gaze slid over her without appreciation. He ran an index finger across his left eyebrow. "You look good enough to eat."

Devour, more like. And not in a pleasant way. Brody Winslow enjoyed sucking people in with his smooth talk and clever charades, and using them up. Once upon a time, that had been her. She'd been taken in by the expensive car he drove and big house he lived in. Not until it was too late did she realize that some of the best liars came from money.

"What are you doing here?"

"I came to collect the money you owe me."

"You've been paid what I owe you this year. Nothing's due for another nine months."

"See, that's where we've got a little bit of a problem. I need the fifty grand now."

"Fifty…" She crossed her arms over her chest so he wouldn't notice the way her hands shook. "I can't pay you the full amount now."

He looked around her house. "Seems like you're doing pretty well."

"I bought the house through a special program that allowed me to put zero money down. I've barely got five percent equity and no bank is going to give me a second mortgage for that. You're just going to have to wait. I'll get the next installment to you in nine months."

"That's not working for me." He pushed himself off the couch and headed toward her.

She flinched as he brushed past her on his way to the window that overlooked her driveway.

"Nice car. It's got to be worth something."

"It's leased."

He shot her a look over his shoulder. "What about that business of yours?"

She bit her tongue rather than fire off a sharp retort. Making him mad wasn't going to get him out of her house or her life. The man was a bully, plain and simple. And he'd figured out where she lived and what she was doing for a living.

"The business is barely breaking even." A deliberate lie, but it wasn't as if her simple lifestyle betrayed the nest egg she'd been building. For so much of her adult life, she'd been on the edge of financial disaster. Having a bank balance of several thousand dollars gave her peace, and she'd fight hard not to give that up.

"I get it. Times are tough for you. But I need that money.

You're going to have to figure out how to get it for me or times are going to get even tougher for you and your pretty baby sister." He patted her cheek and she flinched a second time. "You hear what I'm saying?"

"I hear."

"And?"

"I'll get you what I can." As difficult as it would be to give up her financial cushion and postpone moving Lansing Employment Agency into a bigger, fancier office, she'd make the sacrifice if it meant keeping Brody out of her and Hailey's life. "Now, get out."

Brody laughed and headed for the front door.

Rachel followed him across the room and slid the deadbolt home before his tasseled loafers reached her front walk. She didn't realize how loud her heart thundered in her ears until Hailey spoke. She had trouble hearing her sister's apology.

"He must have followed me home from work," she said. "I'm so sorry."

"It's not your fault. We weren't going to hide from him forever."

"We've managed for four years."

"Only because he never came looking." Rachel sat down on the recliner's arm and hugged her sister. Hailey was shaking. Her confident, bright sister had been alone with Brody and afraid. "Why did you open the door to him?"

"He followed me into the house when I came home from work. I didn't realize he was there until he shoved me inside."

Rachel rested her cheek on her sister's head. "I'm sorry I didn't get home sooner."

Hailey shrugged her off. "Why do you owe him fifty thousand dollars?"

"I borrowed some money to start up the employment agency." It was a lie, but Rachel didn't want her sister to worry. The burden was hers and hers alone.

"Why would you do that?" Hailey demanded. "You know how he is."

Rachel shrugged. "No bank is going to lend a high school graduate with big ideas and a sketchy business plan the sort of money I needed. Besides, he owed me something for the five years I put up with him." She tried to reassure her sister with a smile, but Hailey had regained her spunk now that Brody was gone.

"Those years were worth a lot more than fifty thousand." Hailey levered herself out of the chair and whirled to confront Rachel. Her brows launched themselves at each other. "What are we going to do? How are we going to come up with the fifty grand?" Hailey's pitch rose as her anxiety escalated.

Rachel stood and took her sister's cold hands to rub warmth back into them. "There is no we, Hales. It was my decision to borrow the money and it's my debt to repay."

"But—"

"No." Rachel gave her head an emphatic shake and stood. She could out-stubborn her sister any day. "You are not going to worry about this."

"You never let me worry about anything," Hailey complained. "Not how we were going to get by after Aunt Jesse took off, not paying for college, not anything."

"I'm your big sister. It's my job to take care of you."

"I'm twenty-six years old," Hailey asserted, her tone aggrieved. "I don't need you to take care of me anymore. Why won't you let me help?"

"You already helped. You graduated from college with straight As and got a fabulous job at one of Houston's top CPA firms. You pay for half the groceries, do almost all the cooking and even your own laundry." Rachel grinned to hide the way her mind was already furiously working on a solution to the Brody problem. "I couldn't ask for more. Besides, once I pay Brody the money, he'll be out of our lives once and for all."

"But how are you going to come up with the money?"

"I'll try to get a bank loan. They might not have been willing to loan me money four years ago when I was starting up, but Lansing Employment Agency has a profitable track record now."

Perched on a guest chair in the loan officer's small cubicle, Rachel knew from the expression on the man's face what was coming.

"Economic times have hit us hard, Ms. Lansing." For the last four days she'd been listening to similar rhetoric, a broken record of no's. "Our small business lending is down to nothing. I wish I had better news for you."

"Thank you, anyway." She forced a smile and stood. A quick glance at her watch told her she'd run over her allotted hour lunch break.

This morning she'd wired her twenty-five thousand dollar nest egg to her lawyer with instructions to give the money to Brody. For the last five years, she'd been paying him ten thousand a year, double what she'd agreed to in their divorce settlement. Reimbursement for a debt she didn't owe. Punishment for divorcing him. No, Rachel amended, punishment for marrying him in the first place.

Returning to the Case Consolidated Holding offices, she slid into her desk and shoved her purse into a bottom drawer a second before Max's scowl peered at her from his office.

"You're late."

Rachel sighed. "Sorry. It won't happen again. Did you need something?"

"I need you to be at your desk for eight hours."

She tried again. "Something specific?"

"Get Chuck Weaver on the phone. Tell him I needed his numbers three hours ago."

"Right away."

As she was dialing, her cell started to ring. Since Chuck wasn't answering, she hung up without leaving a voice mail and answered her mobile phone.

Brody's voice rasped in her ear. "Did you get the money?"

"I wired twenty-five thousand to my lawyer this morning."

"I said fifty."

Demanding bastard. "It's all I could get." She kept her voice low to keep from being overheard. "You'll just have to be happy with that."

"Happy?" He chuckled, the sound low and forced. "You don't seem to get it. I need the whole fifty thousand now."

"I get it," she said. "You've been on a losing streak."

She hadn't known about his gambling until the second year of their marriage. A shouting match between him and his father clued her in to his destination when he vanished on the weekends. Frankly, she'd been disappointed. She'd thought he was having an affair. Had hoped he'd fallen in love with someone else and would ask for a divorce.

"That's none of your business."

"You need to get some help."

"You need to get me the rest of my money." He disconnected the call.

Rachel blew out a breath and pushed back from her desk. She had to clear her head. It wasn't until she stood up that she realized someone watched her. Max wore an inscrutable expression, but his shoulders bunched, tension riding him hard. He had the sexy overworked COO look going today. Coat off, shirt sleeves rolled up and baring muscled forearms. She stared at his gold watch to keep her gaze from wandering to his strong hands, and her mind from venturing into the memory of how gently he'd caressed her skin.

"Chuck Weaver wasn't in his office," she said, burying her shaking hands in her pockets. "I'm going to run to the ladies room. I'll have him paged when I get back."

Max shut off her torrent of words with a hard look. "Come into my office. We need to talk."

At his command, Rachel froze like an inexperienced driver facing her first spinout.

"Just give me a second," she protested, her eyes shifting away from him as if looking for an escape.

"Now." Max strode into his office and waited until she entered before he shut the door, blocking them from prying eyes. "Who was that on the phone?"

"No one."

"It sure sounds as if you owe no one a great deal of money." Her evasion irritated him.

He didn't want to care if she was in trouble, but couldn't ignore the alarm bells that sounded while he listened to her side of the phone call. With ruthless determination, he shoved worry aside and focused on his annoyance. The fact that she was in a bad spot wasn't his concern. Her ongoing distraction from her job was.

"You had no right to eavesdrop on my private conversation," she returned, belligerent where a moment earlier, she'd been desperate and scared.

He anchored one hand on the wood door to keep from launching across the room and shaking her until her teeth rattled. "You seem to forget whose name is on the door."

Her stubborn little chin rose, but she wouldn't make eye contact.

"It's none of your concern."

That was the wrong thing for her to say. "When they're calling here it becomes my concern."

Her defiance and his determination stood toe to toe, neither giving ground.

She broke first. Her gaze fell to his wingtips. "It won't happen again."

"Can you guarantee that?"

With her hands clenched to white-knuckle tightness at her side, she pressed her lips into a thin rosy line. Her nonanswer said more than words.

Frustration locked his vocal cords, making speech impossible. He sucked in a calming breath, keenly aware he was venturing into something that was none of his business. If he had an ounce of sense, he'd back off and let her deal with whatever mess she'd stepped in. Unfortunately for him, below his irritation buzzed a hornet of disquiet. He ducked the pesky emotion the way he'd dodge the stinging insect, but it darted around with relentless persistence.

"Do you need help?" He wrenched the offer free of his better judgment. The ramifications of involving himself in her troubles were bound to bite him in the...

"No." Her clipped response matched his offer in civility and warmth.

They glared at each other. Two mules with their heels dug in.

He should be glad she'd turned him down. Instead, her refusal made him all the more determined to interfere.

"Stop being so stubborn. Let me help you. How much do you owe?"

Her eyes never wavered from his, but she blinked twice in rapid succession. "I don't need your help."

"But I need things to run smoothly. I can't afford for you to be distracted by money problems. I assume that's what you've been dealing with on your extended lunch breaks."

"I've got everything under control."

"That's not the way it sounded just now." Max shoved

away from the door and stalked in her direction. He had no idea what he planned to do when he reached her. Something idiotic, no doubt, like take her in his arms and kiss her senseless.

The scent of her filled his nostrils. Some sort of nonfloral fragrance that made him think of clean sheets bleached by the sun. He was assailed by the image of her remaking the bed in their beach bungalow after their frantic lovemaking had ripped the sheets from the mattress.

His irritation faded. "You sounded upset."

Her eyes widened at whatever note of concern she heard in his voice. "I'm not going to let you help me."

Damned stubborn fool.

He caught her arm and pulled her across the gap between them. She came without resistance, her lips softening and parting as a rush of air escaped her. He wanted to sample those lips. Were they as pliant and intoxicating as ever?

"How are you going to stop me?" he demanded, cupping the back of her head to hold her still.

He dropped his head and claimed her mouth, swallowing her tart answer. He expected resistance. They'd been dancing around this moment for almost a week. The shoving match of his will against hers had inflamed his appetite for a similar battle between the sheets.

She moaned.

Her immediate surrender caught him off guard. It took him a second to change tactics, to stop taking and coax her instead to open to his questing kiss. She tasted like fruit punch, but went to his head like a Caribbean rum cocktail.

Long fingers darted into his hair. Her muscles softened. The flow of her lean lines against his frame was like waves on a beach, soothing, endlessly fascinating. With his eyes closed, the surf roaring in his ears, he remembered how it felt to hold her in his arms.

In a flash, all the memories of her that he'd locked away came back. Every instant of their time together played through his mind. His heart soared as he remembered not just the incredible sex, but the soul-baring connection they'd shared.

Then came her leaving. The ache that consumed him. His destructive anger.

Max broke off the kiss. Chest heaving, he surveyed the passion-dazed look in her azure eyes. Her high color. The flare of her nostrils as she scooped air into her lungs. He felt similarly depleted of oxygen. Surely that was the reason for his lightheadedness.

"That was a mistake," he said, unable to let her go.

Rachel took matters into her own hands. She shifted her spine straight and pushed on his chest. His fingers ached as she slipped free.

"That's supposed to be my line," she said, tugging her jacket back into order.

He inclined his head. "Be my guest."

Max retreated to the couch. Resettling his tie into a precise line down the front of his shirt, he laid his arm over the back of the couch and watched Rachel battle back from desire. She recovered faster than he'd hoped.

"That was a mistake." Crossing her arms over her chest, she leveled a narrow look his way. "One that won't be repeated."

"You misunderstand me," he said. "The mistake I referred to was letting the kiss happen here."

"What do you mean here? There's no place else it's going to happen."

He hit her with an are-you-kidding expression. "You're crazy if you think this thing between us is going to die out on its own."

"It will if you stop fanning the flames."

He had to fight from smiling at her exasperated tone. "Impossible. You set me on fire every time I get within twenty feet of you."

"I'm flattered."

Was she really? Her tight lips told a different story. "Don't be. I'm sure I get to you the same way." He plowed on, not giving her time to voice the protests bubbling in her eyes. "It's just a chemical reaction between us. Something ageless and undeniable. We can burn it out, but I don't see it just fizzling out."

"I really don't have the energy for this," she groused.

"Good. Stop fighting me and conserve your energy. I have a much better use for it."

Her arms fell to her sides. "Max, please be reasonable."

She'd stooped to pleading. He had her now.

"When have you ever known me to be reasonable?"

That wrung a grimace out of her. "Good point." She inhaled slow and deep; by the time the breath left her body, she'd changed tactics. "What'd you have in mind?" she questioned, retreating into humor. "A quickie in the copy room?" Pulling out her smart phone, she plied it like a true techno geek. "My schedule clears a bit at three. I can give you twenty minutes."

Max cursed. He should have anticipated she'd use humor to avoid a serious conversation. "I'll need more than twenty minutes for what I have in mind."

"You want more than twenty minutes," she corrected him, letting her thick southern accent slide all over the words. "You probably don't need more than…" She paused and peered at him from beneath her lashes. "Ten?"

Max rose from the couch and prowled her way. She turned her back as he stepped into her space. He loomed over her in order to peer at her phone's screen. So, she wanted to mess with him. Two could play at this game. A minute quiver betrayed her reaction to his proximity. Tension drained from his body. The chemistry between them was textbook and undeniable. His palms itched to measure her waist, reacquaint themselves with her breasts.

"I wasn't so much thinking of my needs as yours," he said, his voice low and intimate. "I know how much you like it when I take my time."

She sized him up with a sideways glance. "I thought this was the sort of thing you were trying to avoid doing with your assistant."

Max shook his head. "I was trying to avoid losing my freedom in one of your matchmaking schemes."

"You were trying to avoid marriage?" She slipped the phone back into its cradle at her waist. "Or falling in love?"

"Both."

"Because they don't always go hand in hand, you know."

"I'm all too familiar with that truth."

As she well knew. The four days they'd spent together hadn't been limited to learning about each other physically. Max had shared his soul, as well. Whether because they'd been two strangers sharing a moment with no thought of a future, or because being with her had thawed places long numb, he'd told her everything about his childhood and the problems with his family, delving into emotions he had no idea lurked beneath his skin.

She'd been a damn good listener. Made it easy to be vulnerable. He'd felt safe with her. And she'd left him. Gone back to her husband.

What an idiot he'd been.

"I'll go get Chuck Weaver on the phone," she said, retreating from his office.

It wasn't until he sat behind his desk and answered the call she put through that he realized she'd completely distracted him from getting answers about what sort of financial mess she was in.

Four

By six o'clock, the offices and cubicles around Rachel were dead quiet. Executing a slow head roll to loosen her shoulder muscles, she gusted out a sigh and saved the spreadsheet she'd been working on for the last couple of hours. Max had asked her to analyze the operations budget for one of the companies Case Consolidated Holdings owned in Pensacola, Florida. The company had been struggling with profitability for the last five years, and Max wanted her to figure out where they could trim expenses.

Whether Max knew it or not, she was the perfect person to figure out how to cut the fat. Ever since she'd lost her father and taken on the responsibility of her sixteen-year-old sister, money had been tight. She'd learned how not just to pinch a penny, but to turn it inside out and scrape every last bit of value out of the thing.

She cast a glance toward Max's office. Should she sneak out or say good-night? The kiss earlier had rattled her more than anything else she'd experienced in the last seven days and with Brody's unexpected reappearance and outrageous demand, it had been a doozy of a week.

As if summoned by her thoughts, Max appeared in the doorway.

"Leaving?" His low question boomed into the silence.

"It's six o'clock. We're the only ones here." She gulped as her words registered.

Pointing out to him that they were completely alone was probably not the brightest move after what happened between them today. The discovery that he intended to rekindle their affair made maintaining her cool a big challenge. If he'd decided this would be the perfect time to assault her willpower, it wouldn't be much of a skirmish.

That he still wanted her both worried and excited her. The heat between them remained as fierce as ever, and as much as he seemed to despise her for not being truthful five years ago, he was right when he said the passion between them hadn't been allowed to run its course back then.

Their four days together had been like an appetizer. One of those fancy ones that awakened the palate, but when you finish sampling, you're still hungry.

How long would the main course last?

A month?

Two?

Max leaned his shoulder against the door frame and regarded her through narrowed eyes. "I thought maybe we could have dinner and discuss your problem."

Translation, he wanted to probe her for more information about the phone call with Brody he'd eavesdropped on.

"You're the only problem I have," she muttered.

"I sincerely doubt that."

Rachel decided to let his remark pass unchallenged. "I can't have dinner with you. I have plans."

"A date?" His smooth tone gave away nothing, but his gaze gained an edge as he awaited her answer.

"Dinner with my sister." Why Rachel felt compelled to assure him she wasn't seeing anyone, she had no idea. Max wouldn't care if she was involved with someone. As long as she wasn't married, in his mind she was fair game. "She does all the cooking at home so I take her out once a week as a treat."

"I seem to recall she was in college when we first met. Did she graduate?"

"Right on schedule." Pride coated Rachel's voice. She might have done a lot of things wrong in her life, but somehow none of it had tainted Hailey. She'd turned out just fine. "She works for a CPA firm not far from here. Between work and her boyfriend, she's pretty busy, but we always make time one night a week."

An invitation to join them tickled the end of her tongue. Hailey would love to meet Max. Her sister fussed over Rachel's lack of a social life as if it was the worst thing in the world and would be giddy to know she'd spent four days in Gulf Shores, Alabama, having the most amazing sex of her life with a hottie like Max Case.

"I'll bet she's not as busy as you."

Was that a note of admiration in his voice? Rachel gripped her purse strap and fought the impulse to cross the five feet of space that separated them and smash her body against his. A throb of need pounded through her. Longing tightened her chest. Her breath grew shallow. If she met his gaze would she risk standing up Hailey for the first time ever?

His next words answered her question.

"Have a nice evening."

With her emotions a muddle of disappointment and relief, Rachel stood by her desk and watched him disappear into his office. Breathing became easier with him gone. Rachel muttered a curse.

She was way too infatuated with Max's tall, solid frame, smoky gray eyes and devilish smile for her own good. But as compelling as his sexy looks were, she could guard her heart against his outward charms. Her marriage to Brody had taught her that beauty was only skin deep.

A strong work ethic was another matter. His dedication to Case Consolidated Holdings touched a chord in her. A workaholic herself, she understood the need to put in long hours. It made her like him.

Which led her into dangerous waters.

This was bad. She'd been working for Max less than a week and almost every hour she caught herself featuring him in her daydreams. Pressure built beneath her skin every time they occupied the same space. How long could she hope to resist the hunger for his touch? Or should she?

That she'd asked the last question told Rachel it was only a matter of time before she wound up back in Max's bed.

She had to pass his open office door on her way to the lobby. Naturally she looked in as she went by. The image of him rubbing the back of his neck as exhaustion swept his features tugged at her, but she kept walking.

Nearing the elevator, she savagely shoved her thumb against the button with the down arrow. Damn him for getting under her skin. So what if he'd looked tired? So what if he'd been working late every night this week?

She cursed the urge to march back to his office and bully him into knocking off for the day even as she retraced her steps, poked her head into his office and asked, "Do you want to join us for dinner?"

Max looked up in surprise. For a split second, a smile tugged at his lips. "I don't want to intrude." But he was already getting to his feet.

"I'm sure Hailey won't mind." Her pulse accelerated as he advanced across the room. His gaze bored into her, and Rachel fought to subdue her body's reaction to the questions lurking in his gray eyes. "Aren't you going to grab your coat and briefcase?"

"I need to come back and finish up some things later."

A man after her own heart. "Okay."

With an entire elevator to themselves, he chose to set his back against the wall beside her. His shoulder grazed hers. The urge to lean against him swelled in her. How was it that four short days with him had left such an imprint on her body and soul? She knew without hesitation that they could tumble back into bed and pick up where they'd left off without a trace of awkwardness. The kiss this afternoon had proven that. He knew exactly how she liked to be touched. Remembered the precise spot on her back that made her knees turn to jelly.

"I've got a business trip to Pensacola scheduled Friday," he said, his brisk tone banishing her evocative musings. "I'd like you to come along."

Warning bells clanged. She cleared her throat. "Did Andrea accompany you on trips?"

"Rarely."

"Then you don't really need me, do you?" But she wanted to go. Wanted an excuse to spend more time alone with him. She knew the risks, but the thrill of being in his arms overrode prudence.

"On the contrary. You have a reputation for being able to read people. Isn't that how you make your perfect matches?"

Refusing to defend herself against his mockery, she watched the numbers light up above the door and wondered if she could get the elevator to descend faster by willpower alone.

"I could really use your opinion," he coaxed, altering his approach.

Rachel's defenses dropped at his softer tone. A quick check told her he was completely in earnest. Against her better judgment, she let herself feel flattered that he took what she did seriously. Very seriously, in fact.

"I'm really not sure I can be much help," she said as the elevator door opened.

"Let me be the judge of that."

Grimacing her acceptance, she stepped into the lobby. Max joined her after a slight hesitation. "We're walking?"

She pointed straight ahead. "The pub is a couple blocks that way. The fresh air will do you good."

"Fresh air?" he echoed doubtfully.

The hot July sun no longer baked the downtown Houston sidewalks, but heat continued to linger even in the shadows cast by the towering buildings. Rachel and Max strolled in silence toward their destination three blocks away—an Irish pub with great food and a relaxed atmosphere.

As they neared the pub, laughter and loud conversation reached them. Despite the day's humidity, the bar's outdoor seating was packed with business people enjoying happy hour after a long day. Max glanced at the windows, hung with neon signs advertising Guinness and Harp, and then the oval sign dangling over the front door.

"I've never been here before."

"Why am I not surprised?"

Max hit her with a hard look. "What's that supposed to mean?"

"It doesn't really seem like your kind of place. And why would you come all the way down here when you've got Frey's in the lobby of your building. That's more your style."

"And what do you think my style is?"

Snooty. Overpriced. Pretentious. "Sophisticated."

He actually laughed. A surprised chuckle that transformed his features into blinding handsomeness. White teeth flashed.

His gray eyes sparkled like sunshine on water. And his lips…
those gorgeous lips relaxed into glorious, kissable curves.

Rachel almost groaned her appreciation.

"Did you forget the bar where we met? It was pretty low
key." He got a faraway look as if his thoughts went backward
to that moment five years earlier when they had locked gazes
across a crowded bar.

Just like in the movies. Rachel remembered that first jolt
of awareness from twenty feet away. Of course, it had been
nothing compared to the sizzle when he'd come over and
leaned close to tell her his name. Goose bumps broke out at
the memory. Two hours later they'd been in his hotel room
ripping each other's clothes off. She'd never experienced a
moment that intense or right with anyone else.

"The food is great here," she said. "The pints are cold.
What more do you need?"

Max opened the heavy wood door for Rachel. As she
passed, he asked, "Does your sister know about us?"

Us?

Rachel's heart stopped at Max's use of the pronoun.

Inside the pub's front door was a small foyer that led to a
second set of doors. The space kept the sultry outside from
infiltrating the air-conditioned inside. Rachel paused between
the doors and took advantage of the quiet to answer Max.

"Are you asking does she know that I had a four-day affair
with you that ended badly and that you've bullied me into
working as your assistant?"

"Yes."

"No."

"Hmmm." Max reached past her for the inside door
handle. His body bumped against hers and started a water-
fall of sparks running down her spine.

"What does that mean?" She stopped and half turned to
confront him.

"It means you keep a lot of stuff to yourself."

She knew he referred to the fact that she hadn't mentioned her marital status to him five years ago. Despite knowing he had a right to be furious about that, his censure stung. "And what's wrong with that?"

"People get hurt."

People or him?

Don't be silly. They'd known each other four days. Not long enough to develop deep feelings. It had been abundant chemistry that had made those four days sizzle. Sure, there'd been some sort of connection above and beyond the physical, but no one fell in love in four days.

"If I don't share everything that's only because I'm doing what I think is best." And she'd kept some whoppers from Hailey. Stuff that if it came out, her sister would be upset. Rachel didn't like keeping Hailey in the dark. She did it to protect her.

"Best for whom?"

Before Rachel could answer, the door behind them opened and three guys in their mid-twenties appeared in the doorway, their good cheer shattering the tension in the small space and forcing Rachel and Max to move forward.

She stepped into the crowded bar, conscious of Max pressed against her back. Happy hour was in full swing. The sounds of merrymaking bounced off the pale brick walls and dark paneling. The space was illuminated by etched glass chandeliers and lighted beer signs. The bartender waved hello as Rachel made her way past the bar in search of her sister. Hailey worked in the building so she was always first to arrive and secure a table. Rachel found her staking out a booth in the back corner. The noise level improved back here. A dark beer sat on the table in front of her. She stared into it as if reading her future in the mahogany foam.

Rachel stopped beside the table. "Hi," she croaked. "I brought company."

Hailey looked up in surprise, her eyes widening as she noticed the tall figure looming behind Rachel.

"I'm Max." A hand reached past Rachel, aimed toward her sister. "You must be Hailey."

Max's solid torso pressed against Rachel's back. She hummed as delight poured through her veins like warm caramel. Only when she saw the hundred unspoken questions setting fire to her sister's keen blue eyes did she stuff a cork in her wanton emotions.

"Nice to meet you," Hailey murmured, unable to tear her gaze from Max. "Very nice."

Regretting her invitation, Rachel slid into Hailey's side of the booth and nudged her toward the wall, leaving the opposite seat open. This meant she would have the pleasure of staring at Max the whole meal, but wouldn't need to endure the tantalizing brush of his arm, shoulder or thigh against hers.

"Rachel has told me all about you," Max said, shooting a smug look her way.

"Is that so?" Hailey plunged an elbow into Rachel's side. "I'm afraid she hasn't mentioned you at all. How do you two know each other?"

"She's working as my executive assistant."

"Why is she doing that?" Hailey quizzed. "She's in the business of placing people, not taking jobs herself."

Rachel felt the heat of her sister's curiosity. Her cheeks warmed as she glared at Max. "It's just for a little while."

"Rachel knows how very particular I am and offered herself until my regular assistant gets off maternity leave."

His double entendre was a cheap shot to Rachel's midsection. Her stomach clenched. She had not offered herself to him in any way, shape or form. Not yet. She clenched her teeth to contain a hiss of exasperation.

"How are you doing that and running your company?"

"I'm managing."

"Is this why you haven't been home all week?"

"I've been home. It's just been late." Rachel lifted her shoulders in an offhanded shrug. "And I've been heading out early. It only seems as if I haven't been there."

"How long do you intend to keep this up?"

"As long as I have to."

Hailey ran out of questions about the same time as Jane, their usual waitress, set a glass in front of Rachel then smiled expectantly at Max.

"I'll have what she's having." He indicated Rachel's drink.

"A black and tan it is," Jane said.

Hailey pushed a menu at him. "I already know what I'm having."

While Max glanced at the menu, Rachel exchanged a non-verbal warning with Hailey, who merely grinned.

Decision made, Max closed the menu and leaned his forearms on the table. Hailey received the brunt of his attention as he said, "Your sister tells me you're a CPA."

"For almost three years now."

"Is that how long you've been in Houston?"

"We came here a year before that. From Biloxi." Hailey leaned back and framed her glass in a circle made by thumbs and forefingers. "How about you, are you from Houston?"

"Born and raised. Except for the years I spent away at school."

"And what business are you in?"

"My family owns Case Consolidated Holdings. My brothers and I run it."

"I'm familiar with the company." Hailey nodded in approval and nudged her knee against Rachel's. "And what do you do there?"

"I'm the chief operating officer."

"Are you two done giving each other the third degree?" Rachel interrupted.

"Not quite," Max said, his gaze never leaving Hailey. "Your sister has been agitated for the last couple days. Is she in some sort of trouble?"

"Max! That's none of your concern."

Hailey's gaze clung to Max as if he was a knight on a white horse come to save the day. Rachel clamped her fingers around her sister's arm to keep her from spilling about Brody and his demands for money.

"I think your sister wants to tell me what's going on."

"It's not a big deal. I've simply had to postpone moving my offices into a better location." She kept her voice and expression as bland as white rice.

"Why is that?"

"I had a little financial setback. Nothing disastrous. It's something that comes with being an entrepreneur. You should know that. Aren't you having a little difficulty of your own since Nathan showed up? I've been hearing stories of arguments that almost came to blows."

Max blew out a disparaging breath. "It sounds worse than it was."

"Who's Nathan?" Hailey asked.

"My half brother. He came to work for the company a year ago and he's been a pain in my ass ever since." Max sipped at his drink, appearing as if he'd said everything he intended to on the subject.

Hailey rested her elbows on the table and her chin on her clasped hands. "Why is that?"

While Max explained about an acquisition they'd decided not to make, Rachel watched him unnoticed. Max's animation and the multilayered nuances of his tone and facial expressions were vastly different from his older brother's stoicism. His passion had captivated her from the start, stirring her enthusiasm for whatever he was interested in. Like some smitten female, she could sit in silence and let him go on and on just to enjoy the way his eyes glowed with excitement and the way he punctuated his words with hand gestures.

"But enough about me," Max declared abruptly. "Let's talk about your sister. Is she dating anyone?"

Rachel came out of the clouds with a thump. "That's none of your concern."

Max's eyes swung in her direction. "It is my concern." His tone had gone deadly serious. "I'd like a clear field this time."

His intensity roused goose bumps on Rachel's arms. She sat on her hands to avoid rubbing the telltale reaction away and gritted her teeth against the shiver tickling her spine.

"What do you mean a clear field this time?" Hailey asked, leaning forward. "How long have you two known each other?"

"We met five years ago," Max admitted.

"In Biloxi?"

"Gulf Shores."

Rachel squirmed as Hailey went completely still. She should have told her sister something about meeting Max in Gulf Shores. At the time, she didn't want Hailey to know how miserable she'd been with Brody.

Her marriage had been anything but a love match. Brody had offered her security and a way to get her sister through college, not his undying devotion. In exchange, she'd agreed to work as his executive assistant and turn her paycheck over to him. Since he took care of her needs, she had little use for the money she earned working for him.

It wasn't until she signed her first tax return that she got a glimpse of how much money she was making working for Brody's family business. She was earning almost three times what an executive assistant should. Way more than he was paying out for Hailey's room and board. And when she asked him where the money was going, she discovered the sort of situation she'd gotten herself into.

She wasn't in a marriage. She was nothing more than a pawn in Brody's desperate attempt to keep his father from finding out how his gambling addiction had taken over his life. When Rachel found out the truth, she was told in no uncertain terms that she'd better keep her mouth shut or her happy little world would vanish. She and her sister would be back out on the street. Rachel knew that keeping her husband's secret was a small price to pay to keep Hailey in college.

But then, things started to get worse.

Brody grew more erratic. He would disappear for days at a time and when he was home, he seemed hunted. He missed family events and Rachel covered for him, but his parents were relentless in their questions. He came home from one weekend with bruises and admitted that he owed a lot of money to a casino. Money grew tight. They were behind on their mortgage. Her credit cards were declined.

The summer before Hailey's senior year, Rachel had enough. She took off, determined to divorce Brody and figure out another way to pay for Hailey's last year of college. Without cash or a plan, she wasn't likely to get very far. Heading to Gulf Shores had made sense. She'd grown up there. It was home. For two days, she'd hung out and contemplated what a mess she'd made of her life.

Then, she'd met Max. Those four days with him gave her a taste of how love was meant to be. Supportive, deeply connected, full of endless possibilities. She'd been a fool to marry Brody. She'd taken the easy way out of her problems and instead, made things worse.

Brody had tracked her down through a call to Hailey. His arrival had shattered the peace Rachel had found. She'd returned home with him because he'd threatened to tell Hailey about their marriage. Rachel couldn't let that happen.

Hailey would feel horrible if she thought Rachel had sacrificed her own happiness and peace of mind so that Hailey could go to a good college. Rachel was no more going to burden her sister with guilt than she would burden her with four years of college debt.

An awkward silence had settled over the table. Rachel could almost hear Hailey's thoughts as she sifted through the subtext of the conversation.

"I remember that trip," Hailey said. "It was the summer before my senior year. You were really different when you came back. Quiet. Except when you were trying too hard to be upbeat. You never mentioned you met someone."

With Max watching her, his expression a cement wall, Rachel swallowed a mouthful of her drink. "Max and I met at The Lucky Gull and hung out for a few days. It was..."

Rachel's eyes slid sideways toward her sister. She kept her face as expressionless as possible. She'd kept the truth about her troubled marriage from Hailey for the same reason she'd protected her sister before and after their father died. As the big sister, Rachel was responsible for Hailey's well-being.

"Casual," Max supplied, his voice as smooth as butter. "No big deal. We enjoyed each other's company for a short time and went our separate ways."

If he intended for this description of their affair to cause her damage then his aim was flawless.

"Casual," Rachel agreed, increasingly worried that her feelings for Max were anything but.

Five

While the sisters talked about plans for the upcoming weekend, Max tucked into a delicious dinner of shepherd's pie and pondered what the hell he hoped to accomplish by digging into Rachel's life. What was it about her that kept him from just leaving well enough alone? Because as soon as he got her away from her sister, he intended to get to the bottom of what was going on.

Was he looking for ammunition to use against her because five years after the fact he was still angry about being an unwitting accomplice in her infidelity? Sure, he had a hard time letting go of things that bothered him, but he'd only known her four short days. Not enough time for his emotions to get engaged. They'd had fun. Lots of great sex. The connection between them might have seemed real, but it had been a vacation fantasy.

As the debate raged inside him, Max grew less certain of his rationalization.

He'd come away from that long weekend in Alabama a changed man. Before he'd met Rachel he'd been an easygoing bachelor, happy to date a series of women with no distrust of love. After their time together, he closed himself off to emotions and made sure anyone he dated knew he wasn't interested in getting serious.

Until recently, he'd assumed his motivation for doing so was born out of being lied to by Rachel. In the last few days, he'd come to realize it stemmed from the fact that he'd experienced the four most amazing days with her and couldn't imagine feeling that way with anyone ever again.

A shriek went up across the table from him. Max's gaze shot to Rachel. The delight that glowed in her sapphire eyes and flushed her creamy skin rosy catapulted her from merely lovely to truly gorgeous. Happiness banished the shadows masking her eyes. The genuine love for her sister revealed her true heart. She was as beautiful on the inside as on the outside.

Her effect on him put his chest in turmoil. Heart and lungs competed for space in his ribcage. As he contemplated what a foolish move it had been to pull her back into his life, Rachel threw her arms around her sibling.

"Where's the ring?" Rachel demanded, snatching her sister's left hand and frowning at her bare fingers.

"Being sized." Hailey wore a concerned frown as she peered at her sister. "Are you sure you're okay with this?"

"Okay?" Rachel echoed, her pitch lower as excitement gave way to confusion. "I'm thrilled. Leo is a great guy. You two have been dating for two years. Why wouldn't I be okay?"

"Because we won't be living together anymore."

"And you're worried about me being on my own?" Rachel laughed. "Are you kidding? I can't wait to turn your bedroom into a home office."

Whether or not Hailey picked up on her sister's bravado, Max heard it loud and clear. Rachel was thrilled for her sister, but that didn't mean that she was ready for the major change in her life. It didn't take a genius to see that the sisters were tight, or that Rachel regarded her younger sibling as a child she was responsible for.

"Congratulations," Max interjected when the sisters paused for breath. "Have you set a date?"

Hailey answered after a quick glance at Rachel. "November fifteenth."

"So soon?" Rachel sagged in dismay. "There's so much to do before then."

"No, there's not. We're going to have a small wedding, just immediate family."

"But that's not your dream. And you've been saving for a huge blowout wedding since the day Leo asked you out."

Hailey held her sister's gaze, her expression determined. "Leo and I discussed it and we really don't want a huge wedding."

"But that's what you've been saving for. Your dream wedding."

"We want you to have the money."

A-ha!

Max's palm hit the table hard enough to cause plates and glasses to bounce, but the sisters were so focused on their battle of wills, neither turned his way. Confirmation that something was going on with Rachel's finances.

"You're being ridiculous," Rachel insisted, her tone scolding. "I'm not taking your money. You earned it. If you don't want a big wedding, use it as a down payment on your dream house."

"But what about—"

"It's okay," Rachel interrupted, gripping her sister's arm. She followed it up with an emphatic, "Really."

Max leaned forward with interest and pinned Hailey with his gaze. "Why would your sister need money?"

"Quit poking your nose into my business," Rachel said before Hailey could answer. "She has this silly idea that she should repay me for taking care of her all these years and paying for her college. It's ridiculous. I love her. That's why I did it. I wasn't expecting anything back."

There was more to it than that. Max could tell from Hailey's sudden silence and Rachel's fierce scowl.

"If you need money, I can help you out." He'd expected her definitive head shake. "Call it a personal loan. No strings attached."

He couldn't resist adding the latter. The way Rachel glared at him sent his libido into overdrive. He imagined her thinking of all the ways he'd use the loan to gain the upper hand in their arguments, as well as other areas. Her expression had never been more transparent. He studied her, his level gaze causing her color to rise. At last she locked eyes with him. The hard glint in their depths warned him to back off.

Sensing Rachel would continue to deny him answers until he got her alone, Max dropped the matter. Then, deaf to the protests of the two independent career women across from him, he settled the bill.

They exited the restaurant only to discover the day's heat had lingered into evening. Rachel's gaze followed her sister as Hailey headed off to where she'd parked her car. The shadows were back in her eyes.

"She's on top of the world," Max remarked, pacing beside Rachel as she retraced the path they'd taken an hour earlier.

"She's really happy."

Max cursed the strong desire to put his arms around Rachel and kiss her sadness away. "But you're not."

"Of course I am." She adjusted her purse strap. "I'm thrilled."

"For her, but not for yourself."

She wrapped silence around her like a muffler and shot him a look that would have taken down a lesser man.

"Not that I blame you for feeling sad," he persisted. "You've taken care of her all her life. It's got to be hard to let go."

"My feelings don't belong in the conversation."

Impatience rose in Max. Five years ago, he'd found her mysteriousness appealing. Until he'd discovered the reason behind it. How bad were the secrets she was hiding today?

"Why not? Surely it can't hurt to talk to me about what's bothering you."

"Nothing is bothering me."

In other words, she wanted him to back off. Too bad his disquiet over her financial troubles was a pest he couldn't ignore.

"That's not true. You've got financial problems."

She stopped at an intersection and faced him. "I'm going that way." Her finger pointed up a street perpendicular to the one they'd been walking along. "You need to go that way."

"I'm not going to let you walk alone to your car."

Despite the storm brewing in her blue eyes, she smiled. "I walk alone to my car every day. I don't need your manly presence at my side to keep me safe."

"Whatever."

He snagged her arm just above the elbow and stepped into the crosswalk. She resisted his manhandling for three strides before breaking free.

"I don't need you to walk me anywhere."

"Stop being so damned independent and let me help you."

She was breathing hard as they reached the sidewalk on the other side. Frustration poured off her in waves. She whirled to confront him. "I don't need your help."

"How about Hailey's help? Why does she really want to give you—?"

She stopped the rest of his question with an open-mouth kiss that left him reeling. Up on her toes, her fingers fisted in his hair, she plunged her tongue into his mouth in a determined bid to divert his line of questioning.

It worked.

Max gathered her slim form tight against his body. He slipped one hand between their bodies, her breast his goal, when a horn honked nearby, reminding him they were standing in the middle of a city street.

Panting, he raked his lips across her cheek. The heavy air had coated her skin with a fine sheen of perspiration. She tasted salty.

"Come back to my place."

"I can't." Her hands retreated from his back, sliding away from his body with haste. "I have a ton of work to catch up on at the agency."

"Take tomorrow morning off and do it then."

"You don't understand." Heaving a sigh, she shook her head and turned aside. "My boss is a complete tyrant."

Max caught her arm and tugged her back into his arms. "A bear, is he?"

She arched her eyebrows and peered up at him. "Always roaring and throwing his arms around in a threatening manner. It's awful."

"Maybe there's a reason why he's like that."

"Such as?"

"Sexual frustration?"

A golden chuckle rippled through her. "Not possible. You should see all the women he dates. There's a list of them on my computer. All their preferences. Their favorite restaurants. Favorite flowers. Favorite music. Even their preferred jewelers. I think he's getting plenty of action."

At her recitation, Max's grip loosened enough that she was able to free herself and put several feet between them. He hadn't considered that she'd have access to Andrea's files and information about his personal life. Sure, he knew a lot of women. Dated a lot of women.

"Did it ever occur to you that he dates all those women because he's searching for something missing in his life?"

"Ms. Right?" She shook her head, tugged her suit jacket straight and raised her chin. "I don't think that's what he's looking for. He's a confirmed bachelor. No woman stands a chance of capturing his heart." Rachel sent a breezy smile winging toward him and headed away. "See you tomorrow, boss."

Max stood where she'd left him, a sour feeling in his gut. At some point today he'd set his toes on the line he'd drawn five years ago in the sand of an Alabama beach. He'd sworn then that he'd never forgive Rachel for her lies. He hadn't understood the powerful connection between them or his vulnerability to it.

Today, in the face of his compelling need for her, Max felt anger and resentment losing their grip on him. How long before his heart was in danger? The smartest thing would be to cut her loose and stop playing this dangerous game. But his whole body ached at the thought of never again tasting her kisses or hearing the sounds of her pleasure as he drove into her.

Max pivoted and headed toward the Case Consolidated Holdings offices.

Who said he had to deny himself the opportunity to enjoy her body? Making love to her. Forgiving her. Falling for her, even. None of these things would result in the loss of his '71 Cuda.

He'd only lose his bet with Jason if he married her. And that was a trap he could avoid with ease.

* * *

At four in the afternoon, a Pensacola, Florida parking lot was the last place Rachel wanted to be. No breeze stirred the stifling air radiating from the sun-baked blacktop. The sky was a perfect blue, unspoiled by clouds. Rachel brushed sweat from her brow and half trotted to keep up with Max's long stride. The dense Florida humidity made her white blouse stick to her skin. Every inch of her felt uncomfortably damp. Only her mouth was dry. The parched sensation had begun the instant they'd emerged into the harsh afternoon sunlight, and Max had transformed from Case Consolidated Holdings' difficult chief of operations to the charming devil she'd toppled into bed with five years ago.

"That's got them running scared," he declared, even, white teeth flashing in a rakish grin. He stripped off his suit coat and flipped it over his shoulder. "When you pulled out your analysis of their numbers, Carlton got so red in the face, I thought he was going to pass out."

Eyes glued to the large brown hand tugging at the knot on his tie, Rachel told her hormones to settle down. Her chastising had no effect on her unruly body. "Are you really going to transfer operations to the Birmingham plant if they don't bring their costs down?"

Bright shards of silver danced in his gray eyes. "Of course not." With a very un-Max-like flourish, he held the rental car door open for her. This was the most relaxed she'd seen him. "They just need to realize that things can't continue the way they've been going." He leaned his forearms on the door and watched as she tossed her briefcase into the back. "It's hotter than hell out here," he remarked, his gaze sliding over her. "Aren't you going to ditch that jacket you're wearing?"

Not on her life. The last thing she wanted to do was relax around Max.

"No need," she replied, ignoring the way his knowing smile made her pulse jerk. "The car has air-conditioning."

"Suit yourself."

Rachel kept her head turned toward the passenger window as Max drove the car back to the airport, but her attention wasn't on the streets of Pensacola. She was running the last week through her mind.

Since the dinner with Hailey and the kiss afterward, the tenor of their working relationship had changed. Max had become less professional and more friendly. His hand had developed a distracting habit of brushing her arm, landing on her shoulder, or sliding into the small of her back at odd moments. Nothing as overt as her action the other night when she planted a big kiss on him, but the subtle touches made her acutely aware of how sensitive she'd become to his every slow breath, sidelong glance, and nuance of posture.

"Are you hungry?"

Max's question snapped her out of her daydream. A glance at the dashboard clock told her she'd been lost in thought for half an hour. "Where are we? I don't remember the trip from the airport taking so long this morning."

"I thought we'd take a little detour before heading back to Houston."

A detour? What was he up to? She recalled his last question. Did he want to prolong their time together by taking her to dinner?

"You don't need to feed me. I can make it back to Houston."

"About that."

She wasn't sure if it was his words or his tone that sent her uneasiness into overdrive. "About what?" Before long, the sign appeared for Highway 292 confirming her unspoken fear. "Where are we going?"

"The beach."

"Which beach?" she asked.

"Gulf Shores."

She'd known the answer before he spoke. Naturally, he'd pick the place where it all began. He wanted closure. What better way to get that than recreate the fantasy of those four days and let their romance run its course? And fantasy is exactly what it had been. She'd been running from reality. Being with Max then had been a frantic grab at the joy her life had been missing since she'd married Brody. She'd never been happier before or since.

Curses exploded in her mind like fireworks. This was going to end badly for her. Worse than the first time when she'd convinced herself the magic of those days had been all about the best sex of her life. Now, she knew better. Max was a complex man who both frustrated and fascinated her. What she felt for him went way beyond the purely physical. She felt a spiritual connection to him. And when that was ripped away, she would no longer be whole.

"I can't." She surveyed his profile and noted the steely set of his jaw. His lips might be relaxed into a half smile, but he was not in a cooperative frame of mind. "I've got things I need to do."

"What sort of things?" He raised dark eyebrows, daring her to lie.

"Things."

"I thought you said your schedule was clear this weekend."

"I never told you that."

"True. I must have overheard you talking to Hailey about how much you were looking forward to a weekend with nothing to do."

"You eavesdropped?"

"Eavesdropped is such a negative word."

"Listened in. Snooped. Spied. Take your pick." Her accusations bounced off him like bullets off Superman.

"It's not like you left me much choice. Perhaps if you were more willing to tell me what's going on in your life."

Rachel ignored his not-so-subtle dig. "I'm not going to sleep with you if that's what you think is going to happen this weekend." With a disgruntled huff, she folded her arms over her chest.

He took his eyes off the road long enough to show her he didn't believe that for one second. "Who are you trying to convince? Me or you?"

She ground her teeth together because she had no snappy comeback. Already her body was softening in anticipation of the feel of his lips against her skin, his hands finding where she burned for him.

"I suppose with all the dating you do, you're pretty confident when it comes to getting a woman into bed," she muttered, unable to leave well enough alone.

"I'm confident you'll wear yourself out resisting what your body wants." He reached across and took her hand in his, fingers sliding over hers with intoxicating results. He lifted her hand and lightly brushed to his lips across her knuckles.

She sighed at the gentle tug of his warm, moist mouth against her skin. She felt a damp heat between her thighs and resisted the urge to squirm on her seat as he ministered to the inside of her wrist, tongue flicking out to probe her staccato pulse.

"Pay attention to your driving." She used her free hand to pry herself out of his grasp. Much more of that delicious sucking and nibbling and she would put that hand of his where it would do her the most good. "I don't want to get into an accident."

With a low, sexy chuckle, he returned his full attention to the traffic around them.

Even with the air conditioner running at full blast, Rachel felt uncomfortably warm. Since willing her body to cool and settle wasn't working, she peeled off her jacket and released the top two buttons on her blouse. Raking her fingers through her hair, she disturbed the gel she'd used to restrict the waves into a sleek hairstyle. She rolled up her sleeves, took off her clunky jewelry, kicked off her shoes and shed her professional image.

"I suppose I'm falling right into your trap by saying I have nothing to wear but the clothes on my back."

"Normally, this would be where I'd tell you that I intend to keep you naked all weekend." Max glanced over at her, eyes burning with carnal promises. "But I had Hailey pack a bag for you. It's in the trunk."

Her own sister had betrayed her. Rachel's chest ached as she rested her elbow on the door and her head on her palm. "You thought of everything."

"I like to prepare for all contingencies."

Off to their left, sunlight sparkled on the Gulf of Mexico. A familiar sight from her childhood. Rachel flinched away from the sharp stab of nostalgia. Was it possible her father had been dead ten years? She missed him every time she sat in his scruffy old recliner or pan fried grouper the way he'd taught her.

They'd been a happy family—she, Hailey and their dad. Both Rachel and her father had worked hard to make sure Hailey never missed the mother that had run out shortly before Hailey turned two. Rachel remembered her as a sharp voice and little else. Her dad hadn't talked about her and there weren't any pictures of her in the house. The lack of a mother hadn't bothered Rachel until she turned thirteen and realized she didn't know much about becoming a woman. If she'd had a mother to advise her, would she have made so many stupid choices?

"Are you all right?" Max had caught her wiping away a tear.

"The sun's in my eyes." She lowered her visor and blinked

rapidly to clear moisture so she could see. "I wish I hadn't forgotten my sunglasses back in Houston."

Max whipped his off. "Take mine."

"You need them to drive."

"I'll be okay."

"Thanks." She slipped them on, appreciating the UV protection as well as the shield against Max's curiosity. "I'll buy a pair when we stop."

It was an hour's drive from Pensacola to Gulf Shores. Rachel recalled making the trip in reverse with her high school friends in those happy days before her father died. They'd head up to the "big city" to catch a movie or go shopping. There'd been a huge sense of freedom in getting in the car and going.

Her decision to take Hailey to live with Aunt Jesse in Biloxi after their dad died had robbed her sister of those sorts of fun times. If only she hadn't been so afraid to take on the responsibility of supporting her and her sister. At the time it seemed sensible to seek out the help of an adult. Of family. Too bad she didn't know what a loser their aunt was until it was too late.

Max's warm fingers stole over the fist balled on her thigh. "You know, it won't kill you to talk to me."

The soothing slide of his skin against hers caused her to release the breath she'd bottled up. She loved holding hands with him. They'd done a lot of that during those days at the beach. In fact, she doubted they'd gone more than five minutes at a time without touching. When they'd been out in public, most people had taken them as newlyweds, asking if they wanted their picture taken together.

To Rachel's surprise, Max had played along. Despite his claims that he never intended to marry, he'd sure enjoyed playing the part of smitten bridegroom.

What he never knew was that she'd asked one couple to

take their picture and email it to her. She'd stared at it every day until Brody found it on her computer and deleted it.

"I didn't tell you last time, but Hailey and I grew up around Gulf Shores. Dad was a deep-sea fishing guide. The best in the county."

He cocked his head. "How come I didn't know that?"

She shrugged. "You did most of the talking that weekend."

"I guess I did." His forehead creased. "That's not going to happen again."

"Are you sure?" she teased, forcing lightness she didn't feel into her tone. "You're kind of an egomaniac."

Rachel's doubts about spending this weekend with Max were coming to a boil once more. Last time, they'd been able to drop their guards and completely enjoy each other with no reservations or baggage between them. Intimacy had come easy because they'd been strangers.

Max's fingers tightened on hers. "Don't do that."

"What?" Her stomach crashed to her toes.

"Push me away with humor."

"Was I funny? You'd be the first person to say so." Rachel heard herself and ejected a sigh. "You're right. I'm sorry. I've never been good at playing with others." Amusement stirred at Max's impatient snort. "You know, now that I've gotten started, I don't think I can stop."

"I think you can," Max said, all serious. "Why don't you start by telling me why you and your sister left Gulf Shores?"

Max could try to dig up all the details about her past he wanted in an effort to rediscover the connection they'd briefly enjoyed five years ago, but he'd find out pretty quickly that the walls she'd spent the last ten years erecting wouldn't come down without a prolonged siege. And time was something they didn't have. A couple days, a couple weeks maybe, and he'd lose interest in her.

"Our dad died when I was eighteen and Hailey was sixteen. He was shot during a convenience-store robbery in Foley, Alabama. He had a girlfriend up there that he visited a couple times a month. They hadn't been dating long, but I had the feeling he really liked her."

"Had you met her?"

Rachel shook her head. "No, he didn't like bringing anyone around. He didn't want us to get attached to anyone in case things didn't work out." She watched beach houses slide past the window, barely recognizing the area with all the new construction that had taken place, but she knew they were getting close. "Our mom left when we were little. Dad didn't want to set us up to get hurt again."

"He sounds like a great father."

"The best." Remembering there had been tension between Max and his father, she didn't elaborate on all the wonderful things about her dad. "He put his life on hold to look after Hailey and me. I didn't realize how much until after he was dead and all his friends started telling stories of job offers he'd turned down because he wanted us to grow up in a community like Gulf Shores. There'd even been a woman he'd wanted to marry, but she had a big career somewhere up north and he wanted to keep us down here."

"Sometimes there are obstacles to a relationship that can't be overcome."

Like how she'd neglected to tell Max she was married? She probably should have ended things with him when she'd learned about his father's affair. After twenty years, Max couldn't let go of his resentment that his father had loved someone other than Max's mother. Even worse, Brandon Case had loved the child of that union as much as he'd loved his legitimate sons.

"And sometimes people are just plain stubborn. Hailey and I could have grown up anywhere and been just fine. I think Dad was afraid to trust anyone after the way my mom left us."

"Trust once broken is often impossible to heal."

And yet, here they were. Rachel let her head fall back against the headrest. This weekend was going to be a disaster. Why hadn't she pitched a fit until she convinced Max to take her home?

Because she wanted to be with him, no matter the cost to her heart and soul? She was a fool.

"You're right about that," she said. "Especially when people refuse to change." The sun dipped into the clouds looming on the horizon and Rachel pulled off the sunglasses. She handed them back to Max. "Looks like we might get some rain tonight."

"I checked the forecast for the weekend and it promised sunshine both days."

"Forecasts aren't always accurate."

"Let's just say, I'm feeling optimistic."

Was he, now. "Optimistic enough to only book one hotel room?"

Max answered her question with a blazing smile.

Six

Letting her stew about their destination amused Max for the next half hour. The silence gave him time to mull over what he'd learned about her. He'd known she'd taken care of Hailey and helped her by paying for college. It just never occurred to him how young she'd been when she'd taken on the responsibility of her sister.

As they entered the city limits of Gulf Shores, Rachel sat forward in her seat, her expression growing animated. Had she been back in the last five years? Many times he'd imagined her here. Pictured her long blond hair whipping around her face as she walked the beach or sat having breakfast at Jolene's Hideaway.

The car streaked past the beach cottages where they'd spent their four days together. Rachel's gaze snagged on the cluster of pale peach structures, her head turning as she kept her sights locked on them. Curiosity and confusion melded in the turbulent blue depths of her eyes as they came to rest on him.

"We're not staying there?"

"No."

"Then where?"

"You'll see."

They quickly left the main strip behind, hotels, restaurants and shops giving way to beach homes. Leggy structures built on pilings lined the road, their colors pale representations of the surrounding landscape.

"I thought you said we're staying in Gulf Shores," she persisted.

"We are."

"But the hotels are all back there." She gestured over her shoulder, indicating the town now a mile behind them.

"I own a house here." He didn't need to glimpse her expression to know he'd surprised her. Beside him, her body tensed. "I bought it four years ago."

A year after they'd met. It made sense to purchase property since he'd taken to visiting the town once a month. All in the hopes of finding her again. Proof positive that he was a fool. She'd been married. She'd returned to her husband. Yet he'd returned to the scene of the crime like some lovestruck idiot. Over and over.

When it occurred to him that he was behaving exactly like his father's mistress—a woman he despised for her weakness—that he was willing to take whatever scraps of Rachel's life he could because living without her made him miserable, he'd stopped coming to Gulf Shores for three months. But in the end, his longing for her had been too strong.

Naturally, all this was wrapped up in logic and justified by sound reasoning about rising property values and his need for a vacation home. But each time he returned to the beach house, he couldn't hide the truth from himself. He was here because he hoped Rachel would return to him.

"This is yours?" Rachel's question broke the quiet. She'd rolled down her window and a light breeze wafted in, bringing the rhythmic crash of surf and the scent of brine. "I don't get it. Your weekends are filled with racing. Why'd you buy a house out here? It's a lot of money for something you never use."

"I like the beach." More than ever now that she was here. "Let's go inside, I'll show you around."

Max had chosen the house for it's open floor plan and the location, but as Rachel exclaimed over the granite countertops and stainless appliances in the gourmet kitchen, he decided he might have had a woman in the back of his mind when he'd had the kitchen and bathrooms updated.

As they concluded the tour of the main part of the house and headed toward the bedrooms, Rachel tugged her overnight bag from his grasp and marched into the guest bedroom. He saw that she expected him to argue. Why bother when words would have little effect on her? She was afraid of what the chemistry between them would lead to. Oh, not the lovemaking. The hungry look in her eye told him that her desire for him matched his longing for her. But she was worried how their relationship would change after this weekend.

"I'm going to grab a shower," he told her. "See you in thirty."

When he returned to the small bedroom, he found Rachel in the midst of unpacking. She'd also showered and now wore a pale blue sundress that bared her slender arms and showed off her delicate collarbones. Her damp hair lay flat against her head, the bright gold darkened to bronze. Tiny silver butterflies swooped below her ears.

"Nice," he murmured, gaze snagged on the frothy scrap of red satin and black lace laid out beside her suitcase.

"That is not mine." She shook her head. "And I wouldn't have packed it for a weekend getaway with you."

"Why not?" He made no effort to resist a grin.

She rolled her eyes. "Because it wouldn't have lasted more than ten seconds, so what would be the point in putting it on?"

"Try it on and I'll demonstrate the point."

Max gathered her into his arms and dropped his lips onto hers. He'd meant it to be just a hot, quick kiss, a suggestion of what would come later, but she melted against him and he lingered. He tasted yearning and reluctance in her kisses. Both excited him. He couldn't wait for that moment when passion torched her hesitation and she let herself go.

Dropping his hands to her backside, he cupped his palms over her sweet curves and pulled her hard against the unruly tension in his groin. Her shiver told him she was on the verge of surrender. His stomach took that inopportune moment to growl.

A different sort of growl rumbled his throat as she laughed and flattened her hands against his chest to push him away.

"Sounds like the beast is hungry," she said.

Before she could move out of reach, he caught her hand and pressed it over the erection straining against his zipper. "The beast is starving."

For a series of heart-pounding seconds she cupped him, fingers trailing along his length, and Max found his knees starting to give way. But before he could swoop in for a deep, exploring kiss even hotter than the last one, she twisted free and fled out the door.

"Come on, Max," she called over her shoulder, cheeks flushed, her half smile taunting him. "You promised me dinner."

Ten minutes later, her eyes glowed as they drove into the parking lot of the restaurant she'd recommended. Reluctance, eagerness, anxiety and yearning passed across Rachel's features, and Max wondered what memories this place roused. He took her hand as they started up the steps to the enormous deck that wrapped around the outside of the waterfront restaurant. With spectacular views of the Gulf of Mexico, the deck was wide enough to accommodate two rows of tables set for four and a generous aisle between. Despite the heat, families and couples occupied every table.

Weathered wood boards squeaked beneath their weight as Max held the door open for her to enter the restaurant. Once inside, the cries of gulls and the soothing pulse of the gulf gave way to the chatter of the crowd occupying the tables in the enormous restaurant. Walls of windows on three sides provided stunning views of the beach and offered the opportunity to watch the day draw to a close in spectacular shades of orange and red.

Rachel approached the hostess stand and spoke to the woman who was directing her wait and bussing staff with crisp instructions. "Hi, Mary."

The woman looked around and her face lit up with astonishment. "Rachel Lansing. You darling girl. Come here and give me a hug."

At first Rachel looked overwhelmed by the warm welcome, but adapted with enthusiasm.

"Max. This is Mary. She owns the Pelican's Roost. I used to work here back in my high school days."

"She was one of our most popular girls."

"Yes," Max murmured. "I'm sure she was."

Mary lifted a disapproving eyebrow at his dry remark. "Not like that. She was a good waitress. Always smiling. Never got an order wrong and she could charm the crankiest customers. And we get a lot of those during season."

"I wasn't all that," Rachel demurred. "Dad taught me the value of hard work, that's all."

"Yes," Mary said with a sigh. "God rest his soul. So, where are you living these days? The last time you were here was five or six years ago, wasn't it? You were living in Biloxi, I think."

"I live in Houston now. I run my own business. Lansing Employment Agency."

"And is this handsome fellow your husband?"

Color brightened Rachel's cheeks as she shook her head. "He's a client, actually. We were in Pensacola on business."

To Max's bemusement, he resented being described as Rachel's client. But what did he expect, that she'd announce to the world that they were soon to be lovers? Or ex-lovers? Their relationship, past, present and future, was too complicated to be easily labeled.

"Do you want to sit inside or on the deck?" Mary gathered menus.

"Outside." Rachel grabbed Max's hand as the restaurant owner headed off and tugged to get him moving. "Is that okay with you?"

"Outside's fine."

He squeezed her hand and shook off his pensive mood. This weekend was supposed to be about two uncomplicated days of sex, conversation and laughter. No need to muck it up with a bunch of pesky emotions that would confuse things. Keep it light. Keep it casual.

"Everything looks good," he said, scanning the menu with only half his attention. The rest was caught, spellbound, by the whimsical curve of her lips as she set her arm on the railing and peered at the water. "What do you recommend?"

"I'm having the raw oysters, followed by the pan-fried grouper." She leaned forward and whispered, "Don't tell Mary, but it's not as good as my dad used to make." Then, she resumed speaking in her regular tone. "And for dessert, peach cobbler because nobody makes cobbler like the Pelican's Roost."

"Sounds good."

And it was. Thirty minutes later, Max set down his fork after cleaning up every last peach cobbler crumb and exhaled. "Everything was fantastic. Why didn't we come here five years ago?"

"We had a hard time getting dressed and going anywhere," she reminded him with a cagey grin.

That was true. They'd been insatiable. But looking back with a clearer head, he remembered it was Rachel who'd resisted his offers to investigate the local restaurants. The one time they had gone out for dinner, she'd directed him to a town fifteen miles farther along the coast. He realized now that she hadn't wanted to explain being with a man not her husband.

Then it struck him that this was how Nathan's mother must have felt. Always hidden away. Always coping with the fact that she was the dirty little secret in her lover's closet. Max had spent most of his teenage years hating his father's mistress, blaming her for the problems in his parents' marriage. With twenty years of resentment propping up his perception, he was dismayed to feel a twinge of sympathy for the woman.

As he drove back to his house, Rachel's nerves became more and more obvious. She half jumped out of her skin after he parked the car in the driveway and touched her arm.

"How about we take a walk on the beach?" he offered.

"But I thought…?" she began, obviously flabbergasted.

"That I was going to pounce on you the second we got back?" He wrapped his arm around her slim waist and pulled her snug against his side. He had no intention of telling her that his body was revved up to make love, but his emotions were playing sentimental tricks on him. "I thought you'd be more receptive after a sunset stroll."

"How thoughtful of you to consider my romantic needs."
Beneath her dry tone he heard a throb of anxiety.

Max dropped a kiss on her head. "Just shut up and enjoy
the moment."

Her chuckle vibrated against his ribs, easing the tension.
They shed their shoes by the beachside stairs that led to his
deck and stepped onto the warm sand. Fine white grains
slipped between his toes as they strolled along the beach. The
moon had risen early and shone as a narrow, white crescent
against the deepening blue of the eastern sky. Max estimated
it was somewhere close to low tide because they were able
to walk on the hard, packed sand near the water's edge. The
breeze was too light to push the waves onto the beach with
any force.

"Thank you for bringing me here this weekend," Rachel
said. "I didn't realize how much I missed the beach until
now."

"Why'd you move away?"

She paused so long before answering, Max began wondering if she'd heard his question.

"After Dad died we went to live with his sister in Biloxi."
She settled into her story like someone perched on the edge
of a soft couch, too afraid to get comfortable. "Hailey wanted
to stay and graduate with her friends, but I insisted we'd be
better off if we were close to family."

"So, you don't have any family around here? What about
your mother?"

"I barely remember her. She left when I was four and
Hailey was two. Didn't have much use for us. At least that's
what Daddy said." She slipped into a drawl that sounded very
much like the local accent.

That's when he realized she'd stripped as much Alabama
out of her accent as she could at some point since leaving here.

"And you never knew your grandparents?"

"I never knew anyone from Mom's side of the family. Sometimes it felt as if Hailey and I had been left on Daddy's doorstep."

"What about your other grandparents?"

"We met them a few times. They lived in Iowa and came down to visit from time to time until my grandmother got Alzheimer's and had to be put in a nursing home."

This was more of her background than she'd shared before. Five years ago, she'd sidestepped every question he'd directed at her. She'd been so accomplished at keeping the conversation focused on him that he hadn't been aware how little he knew about her until she was gone.

What had prompted her to open up to him now? Was she starting to trust him a little? Trust him enough to tell him about her problems?

They walked west in companionable silence, enjoying the play of rich oranges and purples across the sky. The clear night allowed the sun to glow red for a long time before it disappeared below the horizon. As daylight faded, they retraced their steps.

As peaceful as he felt with a soft, curvaceous Rachel relaxed against his side, the closer they got to his beach house, the more anticipation tightened his nerves into bowstrings. His earlier decision to take things slow now became the biggest mistake he'd made in months. Why had he taken Rachel first to dinner then on this long walk on the beach when they could have grabbed takeout and eaten dinner off each other's naked bodies?

Need tightened his gut as he watched Rachel dust sand off her feet on the deck. Patience snapping, he caught her hand and pulled her into the house.

"I can't wait another second to kiss you," he said, closing and locking the sliding glass door. Putting his arms around her, he tugged her hard against his body.

A breathy laugh escaped her. "Then I guess we'd better get started."

His lips captured hers in a fervent kiss that paid homage to her vulnerability while giving her a glimpse of how waiting had fueled his impatience. She met his demand with no sign of her earlier hesitation. Her arms came around his neck. He cupped her head and held her still for a deep, exploring kiss hotter than any they'd exchanged. She arched her back, pushing her lower half against his erection, letting him feel her urgency.

"Make love to me, Max." She tugged his shirt free of his pants and found his skin burning for her. "The romance has been nice, but I need you inside me."

In complete agreement, he drew her down the hall toward the master bedroom. Flinging aside the comforter, Max stripped off his shirt and kicked off his shoes. Despite the cool air blowing across his naked shoulders, he felt feverish. Kissing Rachel set him on fire. Making love to her threatened to reduce him to ash.

"Max."

He turned at the sound of his name and caught Rachel staring at him, her hand behind her, sliding down the sundress' zipper. The look in her eyes stopped his breath. The uncertainty lurking in their velvet blue depths was gone, replaced by confidence. She looked radiant in the rapidly fading evening light.

The smile she offered him was equal parts bold and encouraging. "Are you going to stand there and watch or help?"

She didn't need to ask twice. He brushed the straps off her shoulders and the dress fell to a pool at her feet. Clad in a lavender bra and matching panties, she stood still for his inspection, her chest heaving with each ragged breath.

"Beautiful." He played his fingertips along her collarbones

and then dragged reverent caresses along the bra straps to the edge of the bra. "Your skin is like silk."

She placed her palms on his abs and fanned the fire banked these five years. But he'd promised himself he'd take it slow. He wanted to learn every inch of her skin again.

Her fingers crept down his stomach, past his belly button to the low ride of his waistband. Beneath the buttons that held his jeans together his erection strained toward her questing touch. A groan erupted as she freed him. His hard length speared at her belly, searching for the soft, hot sheath that awaited him. Before he guessed her intentions, she grasped him in her hands.

Sensation exploded through him. A guttural moan tore from his throat as she closed her hand around him. The years fell away. There was no awkwardness in her caresses. She remembered exactly how he liked to be touched. Before her ministrations could cause a premature end to their fun, he swept her into his arms and deposited her on the bed.

"I get to play first," he told her, rolling her beneath him and pinning her hands above her head.

Her thighs parted as he inserted one leg between them. She bent her knee and rocked her hips, grinding her pelvis against him in a slow, sexy wiggle that short-circuited his willpower.

He captured her mouth with his again, his tongue easing past her full lips to sample the exotic pleasures that awaited him beyond. Frantic mewling noises erupted in her throat as she tugged to free her hands. He released her, having better uses for his fingers than holding her captive.

"Better," she murmured, hands riding his shoulders and back with provocative flair.

Taking his time, he drove her mad with feather-light kisses across her soft, fragrant skin. Inch by inch, he eased his way down her body, revisiting all her ticklish spots and the ones that made her gasp. Five years had gone by, but he knew her body as well as he knew his own. Maybe better.

His teeth latched on to the lace edge of her bra. Tugging at the material caused her to hiss impatiently through her teeth. He buried his smile between her breasts, trailing his tongue up one round curve just above the line of silk. He wrapped his fingers around her straps and eased them off her shoulders, but made no attempt to draw the material lower. Her breath came in erratic pants as he retraced his tongue's path, this time dipping below the fabric.

"You're being awfully darned slow about getting me naked," Rachel complained, arching her back to reach her bra catch.

It loosened, but kept her covered. She pushed hard on his shoulder, rolling him onto his back. He grabbed her hips and brought her with him. The bra fell, exposing her small, perfect breasts.

Max palmed them with a sigh of sheer joy. Her bra sailed somewhere off to his left as he began relearning the shape of her. Already her nipples had peaked into dark buds. Max half closed his eyes in satisfaction at the hitch in her breath as he fondled her.

Below where she sat, his erection prodded against her lavender panties, seeking entrance. She leaned forward and rocked her hips. His sensitive head slid against the silk of her underwear, so close to her heat he thought he might go mad with wanting.

She reached behind her and seized him. Max's mouth fell open in shock at the intense pleasure that washed over him. A groan ripped from his chest as her fingers played over the head of his erection. His focus narrowed to her hand and the acute agony denying himself the satisfaction his body craved.

He pulled her hands away and meshed her fingers with

his. He closed his eyes to block out her happy smile and the passion glowing in her half lidded gaze.

Not one of the women he'd been with since the day she'd left had brought him to the edge this fast. Control had never been a problem for him until Rachel had entered his life. Max sucked air into his lungs, struggling to clear the fog of passion before something happened they would both regret.

"Condom," he rasped out.

"Where?" She sounded as impatient as he felt.

"Front pocket."

She stabbed both hands into his pockets and plucked out a condom. "You came prepared," she said, dismounting.

The bed sagged to his left. Max shoved down his pants and opened his eyes in time to see a naked Rachel rip open the foil packet with her teeth and poise the condom over the tip of his erection. Clenching his teeth, Max let her finish the task without his help while his hands fisted into the bed sheets.

The time for subtlety and patience ended. With his heart thundering a frantic cadence, Max sat up, flipped Rachel onto her back and slid into her with one long thrust.

The perfection of Max buried deep inside her robbed Rachel of breath. Five years was a long time to go without being complete. And complete was how she felt in Max's arms. No other man reached past her defenses and captured her heart the way he did.

"You feel amazing," he said, voice husky and raw as if overused. The timbre rasped against her nerve endings with delightful results. "I'm sorry I didn't take it slower. I wanted to."

"You always wanted to delay the good stuff," she groused, but couldn't hide her smile.

He dropped a kiss on her mouth. "And you were always rushing me."

"Like this?" She placed her feet on the mattress and rocked her hips into his.

"Exactly like that."

But he began to move with her and the incredible slide of his thick length in and out of her body transported her beyond speech. She peaked fast, the climax shocking her with its intensity and duration.

"What the hell?" she muttered as his body continued to move against hers, stronger now. "Where did that come from?"

"Where they all come from."

He kissed her hard and long, the play of his tongue mimicking the movements of his lower body. To her intense disbelief, pleasure began to spiral upward again. Impossible. She was sated, exhausted by the intensity of her orgasm, yet another loomed on the horizon. Max slipped his hand between their bodies, finding the knot of sensitive nerves and plying it to great effect.

"Come for me again," he demanded. "Come hard. I want to hear it."

Faster and harder he thrust. Teeth bared, breath coming in heavy pants, he moaned her name, sounding as if it ripped from deep within his soul.

"Yes," she clutched his shoulders, driving her nails in as another orgasm rippled outward from her womb. "Yes, Max. Now."

And he came. She watched it unfold. Her inner muscles clenched in aftershocks as he bucked against her, wild and ferocious in his release. It thrilled her that she'd done this to him. For him.

He collapsed onto her with a gush of air and rolled them onto their sides. With Max still locked deep within her body, she bound his legs with her thigh, needing to keep them connected as long as possible.

"I'd forgotten how it was," he murmured, his palm damp against her sweat-soaked cheek.

She laughed then. It burst from her like the trill of a happy songbird. "So did I."

Time and self-preservation had dulled her memories of him. Of this. How else could she have gotten on with her life? And now that she'd tasted the amazing passion between them again, how was she supposed to walk away a second time?

When he pulled out of her arms and headed into the bathroom, she rolled onto her stomach and buried her face in the pillow. The sight of so much male perfection had aroused her all over again. She tingled with glee at the thought that he was hers, and hers alone, all weekend.

And after that?

The question clawed its way out of her subconscious and roosted in the front of her mind. Max was never going to marry. Even if his father's infidelity and mother's acceptance of it hadn't given him a sour view of the institution, there'd always been misgivings lingering in the back of his mind. Hesitations that had bloomed into full-blown skepticism after she'd made him an unwitting participant in betraying her marriage vows. Which meant, even if he changed his mind about marriage, he'd never change his mind about her.

Sunday morning, Max leaned his forearms on the balcony railing off the master bedroom and watched the rising sun shift the color of the sky from soft pinks and lavenders to a bright coral and gold. The wind had picked up overnight, and blew against his face, carrying the scent of brine to his nostrils. A jogger went by, nodding to a couple walking hand in hand as he passed. Farther east along the beach, a black lab chased a stick into the surf, bounding into the water with great enthusiasm.

Behind him, Rachel slept like someone who'd spent an exhaustive night making passionate love. He caught himself grinning. He'd worn her out. And she'd worn him out, but not enough to still the thoughts circling and bashing together in his head like bumper cars.

Last night, his mother had called. She was working on the seating arrangements for her thirty-fifth wedding anniversary party next weekend and wondered whether or not he was bringing a date. He should have told her he was flying solo; that had been his plan when he'd first learned his parents were renewing their vows and planning a big celebration.

His thoughts coasted to the naked woman slumbering in the room behind him.

If he asked Rachel to accompany him, the invitation would alter the texture of their relationship. No longer could he pretend that his interest was purely driven by sexual need. If he introduced her to his family, they'd be approaching something that resembled dating. Is that what he wanted?

Five years ago, before finding out she was married, he'd been ready to head down that road. Four short days with her had caused him to consider what his future would be like with her in it.

This weekend wasn't supposed to be about starting fresh. It was supposed to be about settling old business and Rachel seemed on board with that. Why alter course and sail into a storm when the skies before him were a calm blue?

He could tell himself that he was simply taking her for moral support. Both his brothers would be accompanied by their wives, and there was something about the way Sebastian and Nathan regarded him these days that felt a whole lot like pity. As if life was so much better for them. Both of their wives had them wrapped around their slender fingers. With children on the way, they were as trapped as two men could be. So why the hell did they seem so damned blissful?

Slender arms circled him from behind. Against his back, the soft press of Rachel's breasts, encased in thin silk, jump-started his body. Her hands played over his chest as her lips trailed over his shoulder. He closed his eyes, savoring the sweet seduction of her caresses until her teeth grazed the tender skin below his armpit and her fingers dove below the waistband of his pajama bottoms.

Lust surged, but instead of losing himself in sensual oblivion, he caught her wrists to stop the sexy exploration and trapped her hands in his. "Come with me to my parents' anniversary party next weekend."

"I don't think that's a good idea." Her body tensed as he dragged her around to face him. "You don't want your family getting to know me."

No, he didn't.

"My mother thinks I'm bringing a date." He drew a fingertip along her spine and felt her shiver.

She pushed against his chest. "I'm sure you can find someone to take in the next few days."

At her resistance, every bit of his ambivalence vanished. "I asked you."

Bending down, he hoisted her onto his shoulder and strode back toward the rumpled king-size bed, her fists hammering on his back all the while. He dumped her onto the mattress and slid his gaze from her ankles to her well-kissed mouth and stormy gaze. Gorgeous.

He set his knee on the mattress beside her right hip and pinned her in place with a stern look. "And we're not leaving this room until you agree."

Seven

Rachel hid a yawn behind her hand as Max turned the corner and arrived on her street. With her work schedule, she was accustomed to sleeping less than eight hours a night. But usually she lazed in bed on Sunday mornings and caught up on her rest. This Sunday morning she'd been in bed, but it hadn't exactly been lazy or restful.

As they neared her house, she automatically checked for Hailey's car in the driveway. She didn't really expect to see it there. Hailey had been spending more and more time with Leo. It wouldn't be long before they moved in together. Especially now that they were engaged.

Rachel sighed. She was going to miss having her sister around. The years Hailey spent at college were different. Then, Rachel had acted as parent. She'd shouldered financial responsibility for her sister's schooling, worried about how her studies were going, and planned for the future. Now, Hailey was a capable, accomplished woman in charge of her life. She'd taken charge of her dreams. Soon, she would be making plans with her husband. Rachel's role had been reduced to that of loving sister and nothing more.

It left her feeling a little lost.

Enter Max. Was she using him to fill a void? Being with him certainly filled a place inside her that had been empty for a long, long time.

He swung into her driveway and stopped behind her car. He stared through the windshield in silence for a long moment. "I don't want to drop you off and go home to an empty house."

Why did he always know exactly what to say to melt her insides?

"Inviting you in is not an option." She rushed a shaky hand through her tousled hair. "We'll just end up…" She flipped her hand in a circular motion. "You know."

He laughed. Her heart expanded at his relaxed expression and the silver shards that sparkled in his gray eyes. Max happy was like watching the most gorgeous sunrise ever. Just being in proximity to him in his current mood made her feel lighter than air.

"What if I promise to keep my hands off you?"

"You can stay for dinner," she said. "Although, it might have to be pizza because I don't know if we have any food in the house."

"Why don't you see what's there. We can always run to the store."

Rachel got out of the car, amused by the thought of Max in a grocery store. He had a housekeeper to shop, cook and clean for him. She had a hard time picturing him pushing a cart down the pasta aisle and deciding between linguini and bow ties.

"What's so funny?" he demanded, snaking his hand around her waist as they headed toward the side door that led into her kitchen. He crowded her on the steps, his solid muscles bumping her curves in tender affection.

Her body reacted accordingly, awakening to each cunning brush of hip and shoulder. "The thought of you shopping for groceries." She dug her keys out of her purse and slid her house key into the lock. It had been acting up lately so she needed to jiggle it a bit to get the tumbler to align properly.

Beside her, Max stiffened. "Someone slit your tires."

"What?"

Before she could turn around, he was off the steps and prowling around her car like a pride leader who'd had his territory invaded by a stray.

"All four of your tires are flat." His gaze shot to her. Worry pulled his mouth into a hard line. "You need to call the police."

"No." Her mind worked furiously. Brody had sounded more intense than usual during his last phone call, pushing her because the guy he owed money to wasn't satisfied by a partial payment. Did her slashed tires mean Brody's debt had become hers?

"What do you mean *no?*"

Seeing Max's surprise, she scrambled for an explanation. "I'm sure it's just neighborhood kids acting up. I'll call a tow truck and get new tires."

"This is serious vandalism," Max persisted. "You need to report it."

And explain her troubles in front of Max? Not likely. Besides, she didn't know for sure this had anything to do with Brody and his money problems. "It's not worth the hassle. The police won't be able to track down the culprits."

"You don't know that."

"It probably happened in the middle of the night when everyone was asleep so there won't be any witnesses. I'll have the tires replaced. It's no big deal."

Max set his hands on his hips. "Has this sort of thing happened in your neighborhood before?"

"Not to me," she hedged.

"Something's going on that you're not telling me. I don't like it."

"Nothing is going on. It's just some stupid vandalism." Her voice grew more strident as Max continued to press. Rachel gathered a long breath and aimed for calmer speech. "Let's go inside. I need to find someone who can fix the car or I won't make it to work on time tomorrow. And you know how difficult my boss is if I'm late." She tried for humor but it fell flat in the face of Max's scowl.

He took her by the elbow and walked her into the house. Once the door was shut and locked, he pulled out his cell phone and dialed a number. It turned out to be a friend that owned a repair shop. Rachel retreated to her bedroom while Max arranged to have her car picked up and the tires replaced.

Her heart pounded with vigorous force against her ribs as she dropped her overnight bag on the bed. A quick check told her Max was still on the phone. She shut the door and took her cell into the adjoining bathroom.

"Someone slashed my tires," she said when Brody answered.

"Yeah, well, I told you this guy plays rough."

"This is your problem, not mine. Did you tell him where I live?"

"It was that or he was going to beat me up."

Coward. She let her disgust come through in her tone as she said, "You're a bastard for making me a part of your problem. Did you explain to him that I don't have any more money to give you or him?"

"You could ask that rich boyfriend of yours," Brody responded, sounding so much like a whiney six-year-old that it was all Rachel could do to not hang up on him.

How had Brody found out about Max? And if her ex had told the goon about her, would Brody send him in Max's direction next? She had to stop that from happening.

"I already asked him," she lied. "He broke up with me over it, so there's no money coming from him."

"Ask again. Do whatever you have to do to convince him to give you the money."

"He won't speak to me and I'm done talking to you. If anything else happens, I'm going to the police."

"You're a bitch," Brody snarled, changing tactics. "He won't stop coming after you."

"You tell him he'd better." Or she'd what? Rachel's hands shook, making the phone bump against her ear. She couldn't believe this was her talking. But then, she'd never been this mad before, and with Max in the other room, she felt safe. "And if you don't," she continued, "he will be the least of your problems. I'll come after you myself."

Now, she did hang up. And her knees gave out. She sat on the toilet seat until her hands stopped shaking. Then, she returned to the kitchen where Max stood beside her small breakfast table, feet spread, arms crossed, a determined expression on his face.

She ignored his militant stance and peered into the refrigerator. Hailey had gone shopping at some point during the week. Rachel sighed in relief. She couldn't face going past her car's four flat tires right now.

She pulled out two plastic-wrapped packages and turned toward Max. "Steak or pork chops?" she asked with false brightness. Either could be grilled and served with red potatoes and a fresh salad.

"It doesn't matter. We're not staying here for dinner. Grab some clothes. You're coming home with me."

Dismay flooded her. She stuck the pork chops back in the refrigerator, hiding her expression from him. "Steak it is."

"Didn't you hear me?"

"I heard you, but I'm not going anywhere."

"You could be in danger."

"Because my tires were slit?" she scoffed, but very real panic fluttered in her gut.

"Because I don't think it was a random bit of vandalism."

"And why is that?"

"Who'd you go into the bathroom to call, Rachel? I heard you talking to someone when I came in to see if you were all right."

Of course he'd followed her into the bedroom. He was worried about her. Warmth pooled in Rachel's midsection. No one had worried about her since her father had died. It would be so easy to drop her guard and tell Max all her troubles. He would help her take care of Brody. And then he would walk away because when he found out she was keeping secrets from him about her ex-husband a second time, he would be angry with her all over again.

"I was talking to Hailey."

"And you had to go into the bathroom and shut the door to do that?" He scowled. "What sort of fool do you take me for?"

Rachel worried the inside of her lower lip. "I can't talk about this with you."

"Can't or won't?"

She couldn't face the cold fury in his eyes. Her heart worked hard in her chest as the silence stretched. "Both," she said at last, her voice catching on a jagged breath. "It's none of your concern."

His eyes narrowed. "I care about you. Why don't you think it's my concern?"

"Care?" Her heart swelled as hope poured into it. But what did Max's admission mean?

"You sound surprised."

"More confused. I don't know what you expect of me."

"I don't expect anything."

"But you do. You expect me to let you into my life."

"I want to help with whatever's going on."

"I don't need your help."

Frustration built inside him like a sneeze. She watched it pull his lips into a tight line and bunch his muscles. He frowned. He glared.

"You're getting it whether you like it or not. Pack."

This wasn't going well. "No."

"Rachel."

"Look, this thing between us. It's supposed to be about hot sex until the passion burns out. You didn't sign up for providing moral support and I didn't ask for a white knight to rescue me."

"That's what you think I'm doing?"

"Isn't it? After what happened between us five years ago, you admitted you don't trust me. Are you saying you've changed your mind?"

His stony stare gave away none of his thoughts. "The way you've been behaving tonight gives me no reason to."

She couldn't let him see how much his admission hurt. "Maybe we should return our relationship to that of boss and assistant without benefits."

"Is that what you want?" He asked the question in a deadly tone, soft and calm.

Rachel shivered. If she gave him a truthful answer, she'd open her heart up to be hurt. He'd know how much she cared for him, what having him in her life meant to her.

"It might be for the best." She turned back to the refrigerator, unsure her whopping big lie would stand up to his scrutiny.

Max came up behind her and held the door closed. "Might be?" His breath tickled her nape. The sensation raised the hairs along her arm. "Are you saying you don't care if I walk out the door and we never see each other again? Because that's what's going to happen. And if I go, don't bother showing up at work tomorrow. Consider your contract terminated."

"That's unfair."

"Maybe, but that's the way I roll."

"All because I won't let you take charge of my problems? That's ridiculous."

"No, what's ridiculous is that you won't let me help you."

She turned and put her back against the counter, feeling the bite of the Formica in the small of her back. "I don't let anyone help me."

"Not your employees?"

"I pay them to do a job."

"Hailey?"

Rachel shook her head. Crossing her arms gave her a little breathing room as his chest loomed closer. "I've taken care of her all my life."

"Who takes care of you?"

"I do." And she was damned proud of that fact.

His voice softened. "Everyone needs help from time to time."

"Not me."

"Why?"

"Because, every time I turn to someone for help they take advantage of me." She slid sideways away from him putting some distance between them.

"You think I'm going to take advantage of you?"

"Maybe." She didn't really. Of course, she hadn't thought

Aunt Jesse or Brody would leave her worse off financially than before she'd accepted their help, either.

"You can't be serious?"

Fool me once, shame on you. Fool me twice, shame on me. She'd be a complete idiot if she got fooled a third time.

"Given my financial situation, you probably think that it's far more likely that I'd take advantage of you than the other way around." She hardened her heart against the longing to fling herself into his arms and tell him everything. Once upon a time it had been so easy to trust. But she'd learned the hard way not everyone had her best interests at heart. "But I can't take that chance."

"You don't trust me?"

Instead of answering, she shrugged.

Max blew out his breath. "If anyone in this relationship deserves not to trust, it's me."

"I never asked you to trust me," she reminded him. "I'm sorry if I've upset you, but I need to do this myself." She tried a smile. "And what's wrong with that? You and I both know this thing between us is going to burn out eventually. It'll be easier to part ways if I don't owe you anything."

"I wouldn't expect you to owe me."

"I wouldn't feel comfortable taking help without being able to pay you back."

Max wasn't usually, at a loss for words, but he seemed to be struggling with what to say to her now. Rachel imagined he was sorting through his conflicting impulses. Continue to push into her life and become the guy she could rely on, the one who would be there when things got difficult or uncomfortable. Or just enjoy the physical side of their relationship and be the guy that moved on before things got too complicated.

"Do you want me to find someone to come in for me starting tomorrow?"

The way his eyes widened, he hadn't expected her to be so matter-of-fact about ending things. He didn't know how much armor she'd wrapped around her heart or how many times she'd smiled in the face of heartbreak.

"No." He scrubbed at his unshaven cheek and studied her from beneath long, dark lashes. "Get in when you can. We're not done with this. Not by a long shot."

Rachel nodded, her throat too tight to speak as she watched him disappear out her door. For a long time her legs were too unsteady to move. By the time she walked to her large front window and sank to the floor, Max's car was long gone. She rested her chin on the sill and wished he could hear her silent plea for him to come back, take her in his arms and tell her everything was going to be okay.

A half an hour ticked by before she gave up hope. Max couldn't help her because she wouldn't let him. If she was miserable, she had only herself to blame.

Max drove out of Rachel's neighborhood, his gut on fire. He hadn't been this mad since Nathan decided to join the family business a year ago. But at least then, his anger made sense. His half brother had been pushing his way into a family where he didn't belong since their father brought him home twenty years ago.

Max had no real reason to be mad at Rachel. She didn't want his help. So what? She had an independent streak a mile long. He'd known that about her since they first met.

Did he really think she owed him an explanation about the things going on in her life? What were they to each other? Lovers. Casual ones at that. He'd told her they had no future. He'd given her a clear picture of his boundaries. Now he was upset because she didn't need him?

Max gunned the engine and pulled out into traffic.

This was for the best. It would be easier in the long run if they didn't draw out the goodbyes. A clean break. Just like last time.

Only here he was. In deeper than last time. On fire. Singed body and soul by emotions only she aroused. Around every corner, more secrets. More lies. And his need for her showed no sign of abating any time soon.

The next morning he arrived at the office tired and cranky. However, his surly mood brightened slightly at the sight of Rachel at her desk looking just as exhausted. She didn't greet him as he neared, but her tight expression told him she was acutely aware of his presence. To his dismay, he was relieved to see her. Happy, in fact. The sight of her shouldn't lift his spirits. He was still mad at her.

"I told you to take your time getting in this morning," he said, accepting the cup of coffee she held up to him.

"I know. And I appreciate it, but Hailey brought me in."

"Did you tell her what happened?"

Rachel shook her head. "She saw my car and she was no more happy about it than you were."

"Why am I not surprised?"

She appeared so miserable it took all his considerable willpower to keep from sweeping her into his arms and kissing away the worry lines between her brows. Instead, he jerked his head toward his office.

"Come in for a second."

She hesitated. "Is this about work? Because from here on out, that's all I want to talk to you about."

"Yes. It's about work. I have a difficult situation with an employee and I'd like your opinion on how to handle it."

Once he had her inside his office, he shut the door and gestured her into one of his guest chairs. Then he strode to the window and stood staring out over downtown Houston. Behind him, he heard her soft sighs and the creak of wood as she shifted in the chair, impatient for him to begin.

"Last night you said people had taken advantage of you. What happened?"

"You said you had a situation with an employee."

"You're an employee." Max turned and let his gaze catch on hers. "We have a situation."

"I'm a contractor working for you."

"Same difference."

"And nothing about this situation has to do with our professional relationship."

"It has everything to do with my ability to concentrate on work."

"I'll quit."

"It won't change my ability to get my job done. Five years ago, you walked out of my life and never looked back. That's not going to happen again."

"What are you saying?"

Yes, what was he saying? "That I want to see where this goes. And I want to start by learning about your past and your present. Maybe that way we can have a future."

"It will never work between us."

He snorted. Any other woman he'd ever dated would have been dancing for joy at what he'd just offered. He had to pick the one woman more skittish about commitment than he was. "What makes you so certain of that?"

"The biggest problem is you can't trust me."

"And you don't trust me," Max countered, still smarting from that revelation. "That puts us on the same page."

She crossed her arms over her chest. "We're not even in the same bookstore."

"Let's see if we can change that. Tell me who took advantage of you that makes you so skittish about accepting help."

She opened her mouth, but no words came out. A second later, she bit her bottom lip. Max waited while she grappled with what story to tell him and how much to tell. Letting her sort it out without prompting tested his patience, but he kept silent. At last, she seemed to come to some sort of decision. Her breath puffed out.

"Aunt Jesse." She closed her eyes. "My dad's sister."

"What happened?"

Instead of forcing intimacy by sitting in the chair next to her, Max gave her space by keeping his big executive desk between them.

"I was eighteen when my dad died and still in my senior year of high school. Hailey was two years younger. Since our mom left when we were both young, I'd always thought of Hailey as my responsibility. She was diagnosed with asthma when she turned six. The first time she collapsed and turned blue, I don't think I've ever been so scared in my whole life. After that, I watched her like a hawk, making sure she had her inhaler with her at all times. She was my baby sister. I couldn't lose her, too."

Too? Max wondered if she knew what she'd given away with that one word. Her mother had disappeared when she was four. Rachel had felt the loss no matter what she was willing to admit to herself. And then her father died. Max suspected protecting herself against loss had become second nature. Pity the man who tried to break down those walls.

"Who took you in after your dad died?"

Rachel stared at her hands. "No one. I dropped out of school and went to work full-time to make ends meet until we received the money from Dad's insurance policy. He took it out because you can be as careful as anything when you're out on the gulf, but accidents happen. No one expected he'd be shot during a convenience-store robbery twenty minutes from home."

"You never graduated?"

She shook her head. "I got my GED. I needed to take care of Hailey. Only it was a lot more expensive than I was expecting. And I was working all the time. By the time we got the insurance money, I was exhausted and worried about how I was going to handle everything. We had no medical insurance and Hailey's asthma had been flaring up a lot more since Dad died. The medication was expensive. That's when I called Aunt Jesse."

"Was she able to help?"

"She told us to come live with her in Biloxi. We'd have a place to stay while Hailey finished high school. I could work and maybe go to a community college. The rest of the money could go toward a real college for Hailey. She was always the smarter one."

"So, what happened?"

"For a while everything seemed okay. Then one day Aunt Jesse came home and asked if she could borrow Dad's life insurance money for a couple days."

"And you gave it to her."

"It was supposed to be a loan until she got paid at the end of the week. I probably should have said no, but she took us in when we needed help and she was family." Rachel's bitter smile said more than her expression. "She took the money and disappeared. We were stuck in Biloxi with no money, no friends and no family."

Her story would have wrung sympathy out of the most jaded heart.

"Did you call the cops?"

"And tell them what? That I'd lent money to our aunt and she'd disappeared?"

"Did you look for her?"

Rachel shook her head. "For all she was our closest living relative, we knew nothing about her life or her friends. Or, we didn't until people showed up looking for her. That's when we found out she was dealing drugs and had some rather scary acquaintances."

"Did any of them hurt you?"

"No. After the first guy came knocking, we didn't stick around."

"What happened?"

"I had a waitressing job. I picked up more hours. We found a small studio apartment in a relatively safe neighborhood and scraped by." Rachel downplayed what must have been a scary time for her with a single shoulder shrug and a self-deprecating smile.

Max's admiration for her went up several dozen notches. "I'm sorry you had such a tough time of it."

Rachel's eyes hardened into sapphire chips. "It was my fault we were in the mess."

"How do you figure that?"

"Hailey begged me to stay in Gulf Shores. She wanted to finish high school with her friends. But I was too scared about being solely responsible for her to listen. I wasn't ready to be an adult. Don't you get it? I screwed up. If we'd stayed put, Aunt Jesse wouldn't have stolen the insurance money. It would have been so much easier."

"You were eighteen. Cut yourself some slack."

"Life doesn't cut you slack," she said. "Life comes at you hard and fast and you either meet it head-on, duck, or get blindsided. I've promised myself not to get blindsided again."

Yet Max had the sense that something had blindsided her recently. Something that wasn't him. Something she wouldn't let him help her with.

"You said people *helped* you."

"What?"

"Last night. You said people. That's plural. Who else took advantage of you?"

She offered him a sad smile. "Sorry. I only reveal one major mistake from my past at a time. Tune in next week for the continuing saga of Rachel Lansing's journey into bad judgment."

"Don't shut me out. I want to know everything about you." Max hated the way she kept deflecting his questions. It created a chasm between them when all he wanted was to get close to her. "You know you can trust me."

"Of course I do. It's just that I get depressed when I think about all the mistakes I've made. Can't we talk about something else?"

As much as he wanted to push harder, he recognized the stubborn set of her mouth and knew they would only end up fighting if he bullied her for answers.

He tossed a file across the desk toward her. "Take a look at the Williamsburg numbers in their strat plan. They don't add up. I didn't have time to check it over this weekend and I'm supposed to be on a conference call with them at eleven."

Her relief at being back on professional footing was so palpable she might have stood up and given a double fist pump. Max watched her head out of his office, a slim silhouette in her long pencil skirt and fitted jacket. He wanted to take her in his arms and promise he wouldn't let her down the way others in her life had. But was that something she'd believe when he wasn't sure himself if it was something he could deliver?

Eight

Rachel sat down at her desk and opened the file she'd been working on before Max summoned her into his office. The numbers blurred on the page. She sat back and rubbed her eyes, then reached for her tall coffee with the three shots of espresso. Max was a bad influence on her in more ways than one.

What had possessed her to tell him about Aunt Jesse?

She owed him no explanations. The intimacy they'd developed was physical, not emotional. Yet, she couldn't deny that sharing the story had lifted a little weight off her shoulders. Not much, but enough to help her get through the day. To clear her mind for how she would handle things with Brody. She simply had to find the twenty-five thousand she still owed him.

You could borrow the money from Max. If you asked, he'd help.

And have to explain to him about Brody and why she'd

married him. As if his opinion of her wasn't bad enough already, Max could add opportunist and user to her list of flaws. Besides, she didn't want her ex-husband to come between them again. Although, at the rate she was screwing things up on her own, it wouldn't matter what she told Max. Given the way their conversation had gone last night, he was probably done with her right now.

Rachel made notes on the file Max had asked her to look at and checked in with Devon to see if anything had come up. He was proving to be a great manager despite his reservations about taking on the responsibility. Maybe this meant she could take a long weekend for herself after everything was over. Four days with nothing to do and no worries sounded like heaven.

But was it reality? Since coming to work for Max, she'd been drifting in a fantasy world. The time for daydreams was over.

Right at eleven, Max's conference call began with the general manager of their Williamsburg operations. While he was asking the questions she'd posed about their numbers, his second line lit up. Rachel answered the call. It was Andrea.

"How are things going?" Rachel winced in sympathy at the loud cries in the background.

"As well as can be expected with a baby who's up all hours of the night with colic."

"I hope things get better soon."

"Me, too."

"Max is on a conference call at the moment. Do you want me to have him call you?"

A long pause preceded Andrea's response. "No. I'll try him again later."

Rachel picked up on the other woman's change of tone. "Is something wrong?"

"Not wrong." But something was up. Rachel could hear it in Andrea's voice.

"Anything I can help you with?"

"Look, I don't exactly know how he persuaded you to fill in for me, but you should probably find someone to take over on a permanent basis."

"You're not coming back?"

"Ned and I discussed it on and off since the middle of my pregnancy. Max is great, but he works such long hours." Andrea tried for cheerful but her tone fell flat. "Now with Ben not sleeping, I'm even more exhausted than I was before he was born. We just think it would be better if I stayed home for his first year. Maybe longer if we decide to get pregnant again right away."

"That makes sense to me." Rachel's mind raced. She needed to call Devon right away about possible candidates for a permanent position. "You have to make your family your priority." If anyone understood that, she did.

Andrea's laugh released some of her tension. When she spoke next, she sounded less like she was carrying fifty pounds of salt on her shoulders. "Thanks, Rachel. I hope Max hasn't been too hard on you. I know what he's like when things don't go exactly to his plan."

"Well, don't worry about that anymore. You just concentrate on that baby of yours. He's the important one."

"Thanks."

Rachel ended the call and dialed Devon, giving him the heads-up that they were now dealing with a permanent placement.

"What are you up to now?" a deep voice demanded from behind her.

Rachel glanced over her shoulder and spied Max standing in his doorway. Her pulse jumped as it always did when he was around. He had an annoying habit of sneaking up on her.

"I've got to go," she said to Devon, and hung up. She glanced toward the phone and noticed his line was no longer lit up. "That was a short conference call."

"After I used your notes to point out to them where their numbers still weren't good enough, they decided to go back and reassess. We're scheduled to talk this afternoon. Who was that on the phone?"

"Devon. Andrea called a few minutes ago. She's not coming back. We've got three candidates for you to interview."

His gaze swept her features, settled on her mouth for a moment longer than the rest, then reconnected with her eyes. "How fast can you get them here for interviews?"

"It would go faster if I could work from my office. I need access to my files. My notes. Those are at my office."

"Then go."

And just like that it was over. His abrupt dismissal left her floundering in dumbfounded silence.

What was it about Max that turned her from a hardheaded business woman into a sentimental fool?

A lean, muscular body made to drive a woman mad in bed.

A personality that was one-third angry bear, one-third stubborn mule and one-third cuddly tiger.

But it was the way he looked at her as if she was the only woman he'd ever desired that turned her insides to mush. How could she help but fall under his spell?

It was a short three blocks back to the building that housed Lansing Employment Agency, and Rachel used the time to gather her scattered emotions into a nice neat ball. Sharp pains began in her stomach as she swallowed the desire to cry or shout out her unhappiness. Max was done with her. What had she expected? A tearful goodbye?

Devon was on the phone as she went past his office. Knowing he would be full of questions, she took a deep breath and tucked all emotion away.

"What are you doing here?" he asked from her doorway moments after she dropped into her executive chair. "Did you quit or did we get fired?"

"Neither." After playing assistant for Max these last four weeks, she'd forgotten how wonderful it felt to be the one in charge. "Max wants to interview potential candidates as soon as possible. It'll go faster if I'm here."

"You're on the verge of netting us another big commission and yet you don't look happy."

"Of course I'm happy."

But to her intense dismay, tears filled her eyes. Devon stared at her in stunned silence, before rushing in and kneeling beside her chair.

"What happened? Was it Max? Did he upset you? Do you need me to go kick his ass?"

The thought of five-foot, nine-inch Devon kicking anyone's ass, much less Max's, made her chuckle. Shaking her head, she straightened her shoulders and shook off her melancholy.

"No. Nothing like that. I did something really stupid."

"I don't believe that for a second. You're one of the most savvy businesswomen I've ever met."

"I slept with Max."

"Ah," Devon said cautiously.

"What do you mean, *ah?*"

"I'm not surprised, that's all. You said you'd known him before. So what happened?"

Telling Max about Aunt Jesse earlier today had caused a crack in her self-imposed isolation. She'd felt better, lighter, after sharing her struggles in the aftermath of her father's death. Drawing on Max's strength had helped make the memories less painful. No matter how much she isolated herself, she wasn't alone. Telling Devon about Max could provide the same sense of relief.

"He and I met five years ago in Alabama."

The whole story poured out of her. She explained about her affair with Max. She talked about her financial problems with Brody. She told Devon about keeping everything from Hailey and about her slashed tires. Max's offer of help and her subsequent refusal.

"I understand everything," Devon said. "Except the part where you won't tell Max about the trouble your ex-husband is causing."

Rachel dabbed at the tears that had overflowed onto her cheeks. "My being married to Brody is what caused Max to despise me the last time. I don't want him involved in case Brody sets the loan shark on him."

"So, all your problems stem from the fact that you're trying to keep your sister and Max from worrying about you and pushing them away in the process."

"That's not fair."

"But it's what you're doing."

"So, what am I supposed to do? Explain to Hailey that I stayed married to Brody even though he was stealing from me to pay his gambling debts? That I was then so desperate to get free that I let myself agree to a ridiculous divorce agreement that compelled me to pay back the hundred thousand dollars it cost for her college education? And that I'm being harassed by Brody and whatever goon he owes money to?"

"For starters."

"I can't. I've spent my entire life protecting her. Don't ask me to stop now."

Devon shook his head. "She was a kid back when all the bad stuff happened. She's an adult now. Tell her the truth and let her be someone you can lean on."

"She's getting married. She's starting a fresh new life." Rachel shook her head and dried her eyes. "I don't want her to have to worry about the past."

Devon blew out a breath. "I can see why Max got angry with you."

Despite his neutral, slightly sad tone, Rachel felt as if she'd been slapped. "He wanted nothing from our relationship except sex."

That was a cop-out. She didn't really believe that's all she and Max had. But it was more comfortable to cling to that notion than to open herself up to hope and end up getting hurt.

"He invited you to his parents' anniversary party."

Part of her longed to believe Devon's optimistic take on her and Max. Spending time with him made her happier than she'd ever been. But he'd insisted from the start that he wasn't with her for the long term. And his track record bore that out.

"He's between women at the moment."

Devon stared at her for a long time. "Or maybe he's found the one he wants."

"Or maybe," she countered stubbornly, "he hasn't. And he just likes to stick his nose in where it doesn't belong."

"You don't really believe that's all there is to it."

"I can't afford to believe anything different." Despair was close to swallowing her unsteady composure.

"So, you're going to push him away?"

Rachel picked up her pen and twirled it. "After what happened last night and today, I don't think I'm going to have to."

To her surprise and despite their rocky week, when Saturday night rolled around, Rachel found herself at Max's side as they ascended the steps of his parents' home in the western suburb of Houston, a gated community with wall-to-wall mansions. She had no clear idea how she had arrived at this moment. Sure, she'd given her grudging acceptance that morning in Gulf Shores so he'd stop torturing her body with seductive caresses that got her motor revved up, but took her nowhere.

But after their argument at her house and how disinterested he'd been about her leaving Case Consolidated Holdings…

She figured he was done with her.

Then late Wednesday night, he'd shown up at her office with the sea glass bracelet he'd bought her five years earlier. When she'd gone back to Mississippi, she'd left the bracelet behind because it was a talisman representing hope and joy. By returning to her marriage, she didn't believe she deserved such a keepsake.

She couldn't stop wondering why Max had kept the bracelet all these years. Did it mean he'd never stopped caring about her? What if it had no significance at all? Every question battered the armor surrounding her heart. Sleep came only after hours of tossing and turning. Her appetite had dropped off. She caught herself daydreaming at work while Devon worked harder than ever.

And Brody called her often to remind her how impatient he was.

Her life felt like it was spinning out of control and she wasn't sure how much longer she could hang on.

"Stop fidgeting," Max advised. He set his hand at the small of her back, his touch soothing. "You look fine."

Rather than let him see how ragged her emotions were, Rachel retreated into sarcasm. "Fine?" She glazed the word with contempt. "What makes you think any woman wants to be told she looks fine?"

To her intense annoyance, his lips twitched. His relaxed

mood made it hard to keep her glare in place. Why did the man have to make her so damned happy?

"You look gorgeous."

Her harrumph resulted in a full-blown grin.

"I really shouldn't be here," she said for about the hundredth time. "This isn't a business associate or a group of friends, this is your family."

He'd never given her a satisfying answer about his true motive for badgering her to accompany him. In the end, she'd let him convince her to attend the party, but dug in her heels when he insisted she also be there for the family-only renewal of vows that had taken place earlier that afternoon at the church where his parents had originally been married.

"You're here because I didn't want to go through this alone."

His explanation made perfect sense. She was a stand-in because he was between women. She knew better than to call them girlfriends. Max dated, but he didn't get involved. Casual affairs were more his style.

So, what were they doing?

Since Wednesday, she'd gone home with him after work and spent the night at his house. They watched TV. They made dinner. They made love. Playing house. Getting to know each other better with each hour that passed. The chemistry wasn't burning out the way he'd said it would. In fact, it was getting hotter by the day.

Nor was either of them trying to cool things off or slow things down.

Two months, she kept telling herself. That's how long his relationships usually lasted according to the notes in Andrea's computer. She wouldn't think any further into the future than that.

A maid opened the front door as they approached. The grand, two-story foyer Max nudged her into was half the size of her house. She gaped like a girl from a small beach town. Meeting wealthy executives at their offices didn't prepare her for the reality of what money could buy.

"Did you grow up here?" she asked, trying to imagine three energetic boys roughhousing around the expensive furniture and exquisite antiques.

"No. Mom and Dad downsized after they kicked the chicks out of the nest."

Her breath rushed out. "Downsized?"

"This house only has four bedrooms."

"Only." Apparently, her answers were limited to two syllables.

"Come on. Let's go congratulate the happy couple." The mischief vanished from his eyes as he steered her deeper into the house.

With Max's arm around her waist, Rachel floated through the large, perfectly decorated rooms in a haze of anxiety and awe. Her nervousness was tempered by a couple things. First, the beige silk cocktail dress she'd splurged on might have come off the rack of her favorite consignment store, but it was a designer original and she needed that boost of confidence as they passed by women wearing thousands of dollars worth of gowns and jewelry. Second, most of the furniture had been upholstered in tones of cream, beige and gold. That meant she could sit down and virtually disappear.

"There's Mom. Let me introduce you."

She hung back as Max leaned forward and kissed his mother on the cheek. Dressed in a beaded cream gown with diamonds at her ears, wrist and around her neck, Susan Case looked every inch a wealthy socialite, but the smile she beamed at her son looked warm and genuine enough to put Rachel at ease.

"Mom, this is Rachel Lansing. Rachel, my mother, Susan."

Rachel stretched her lips into a smile, hoping her nerves didn't show, and shook the soft hand Susan Case offered. "It's really nice to meet you," she said. "Max talks about you a lot."

"Have you two been dating long?"

"Oh, we're not dating," Rachel insisted in a rush. "I own an employment placement service. I'm helping him find an assistant to replace Andrea."

"I see." But it was obvious she didn't.

Rachel didn't miss the curious glance Susan sent winging toward her son. Beside her, Max radiated displeasure. Well, what did he expect? That she was going to explain the complicated arrangement between them when she wasn't exactly sure how to define it herself?

"How is the hunt for a new assistant going?"

"He's turning out to be a difficult man to please." She shot Max a warning look to shut down whatever protest he was about to make.

"Is he, now," Susan murmured wryly. "Well, I'm sure you'll figure out how to make him happy."

Rachel flushed at the subtext of Susan's remark and wished a sinkhole would develop beneath her feet. Before she mustered a response, a tall man with dove-gray eyes stepped into the trio's circle and wrapped a possessive arm around Susan.

"Good evening." Brandon Case extended his free hand to Rachel. "My son is lucky to have such a lovely companion this evening."

Rachel smiled at Brandon Case as she shook his hand, unable to stop herself from basking in the man's charm. At her side, Max stiffened slightly.

"Congratulations on your thirty-fifth anniversary," she said. Max's tension heightened her own anxiety and the next words that came out of her mouth, she wished back immediately. "What's your secret?"

Susan dipped her head in acknowledgement. "To a long marriage?" She gazed up at her husband. A gentle smile curved her lips. She was obviously very much in love with the man she'd married. "I think you need to be able to forgive each other and laugh together."

Such simplicity took Rachel's breath away. Was that really all there was to it? She thought about her own marriage. She and Brody had failed at both. She couldn't recall a single time when they'd laughed together. In the beginning, they'd gotten along, but it had never been joyful the way it was with Max.

A slight indent had developed between Max's brows at his mother's words. "And that's it? All the pain just magically melts away? Trust is restored with a chuckle?"

Rachel put her free hand on Max's arm and squeezed in sympathy. She'd been so busy thinking about herself this week, she hadn't considered how hard this renewal of vows and anniversary celebration would be on Max. He'd never gotten over his father's infidelity. And now she saw that he was also angry with his mother for staying with a man who'd betrayed her.

"Of course not," Brandon retorted, his gray eyes hard as they rested on his son. "What I did to your mother wasn't forgiven overnight. It took years before she began to trust me again. And now that she does, I would never do anything else to hurt her."

"Max, this is a party," his mother said, her voice showing no signs of stress. "My anniversary party. Please behave."

As the tableau played out before her, Rachel had a hard time swallowing past the lump in her throat. Seeing Max's expression darken and knowing why he was so upset made her realize she'd been a fool to wonder if the passion they shared might lead to something more.

If twenty years had passed without him forgiving his parents their shortcomings, she'd been a fool to hope he would ever forgive her.

Laughter and forgiveness.

His mother was kidding herself. For years she'd turned a blind eye to her husband's second life with the woman he couldn't bring himself to live without. She should have included sacrifice in the mix of ingredients that kept a marriage going. Because, in his opinion, if she hadn't sacrificed her pride, her self-confidence, and her peace of mind, she would have divorced Brandon a long time ago. Instead, her husband had violated her trust with his infidelity and yet she'd stayed.

She'd stayed because she loved him.

And she'd taught Max a valuable lesson about trust, marriage and love. He wouldn't make his mother's mistakes. He wouldn't trust. He wouldn't marry. He wouldn't love.

The first two he could control. It was the last that worried him.

Coming here tonight with Rachel brought home his own weakness. He'd grown preoccupied with a woman who behaved like his father, keeping secrets, sharing only the surface of her life, not the emotions that drove her actions. How could he trust her? What hidden bombs lurked beneath her composed exterior, waiting to detonate at the worst possible time?

A couple weeks ago he'd wagered an extremely valuable car that he wouldn't marry. Falling in love had been the furthest thing from his mind. But that's before Rachel had brought up all the unresolved issues between them. Telling himself that it was nothing more than passion that needed to run its course was a speech he was having a harder and harder time selling. What he felt for her ran deeper than desire. It had sunk its claws into his soul.

He couldn't control his fierce need for her. Just like his father couldn't control whatever had made him stay married to one woman and love another for more than twelve years. Max had become just like his father. He'd grown up despising Brandon because he'd let his emotional need for Nathan's mother damage his marriage, and in Max's eyes, destroyed his credibility and his character.

Her hand slipped into his to draw him along to the buffet. The simple contact tugged his pulse into a sprint.

Being with Rachel made a mockery of his principles. Yet the idea of walking away was sheer agony. He'd believed the only solution would be to purge his need for her. And the only way he knew to do that was to keep her in his bed until he grew tired of her.

Who was he kidding? He grew more attached to her every day.

On their way to the backyard where a dining tent had been set up to accommodate the guests, they were intercepted by a dateless Jason.

"I don't believe we've met." Max's best friend took Rachel's hand and bent forward to smile into her eyes. "I'm Jason Sterling, and you are way too gorgeous to waste your time on my friend here."

Max stiffened at his friend's flirtatious manner. They'd competed over women a time or two, but once either staked his claim, the other immediately backed off. A growl started building in Max's chest as Jason's gaze dropped from Rachel's face to scope out the rest of her.

"Rachel Lansing," she said. "I know your father. How are he and Claire doing?"

"They're doing great, thanks to you. My father's never been happier." Jason's keen eyes surveyed them. "Are you two dating?" A vile grin curved his lips as he looked to Max for confirmation.

"Something like that." Max stared down his friend, warning Jason to keep further comments to himself, and slid his hand into the small of Rachel's back.

Jason looked positively delighted. "How long has this been going on?"

"We're just old friends," Rachel said, offering her own version of their relationship.

"Are you, now?" Jason looked entirely too pleased with himself as he turned to Max. "I got an offer on my '69 Corvette yesterday. Looks like I should take it. I have a feeling there's a new car in my near future."

The taunt infuriated Max. "I've got room in my garage for the 'Vette. Maybe I'll take it off your hands."

Jason just laughed and turned his charm back on Rachel. "Will you sit next to me at dinner?"

"She's with me," Max growled.

"I thought you two were just old friends."

Max stepped between Rachel and Jason, bumping his best friend in the process. "You're supposed to bring a date to events like this, not poach someone else's." It wasn't until he'd settled Rachel at the table and taken his place beside her that his annoyance with Jason dulled to a nagging irritation.

Snarling like a guard dog was not the usual way he kept other men from sniffing around his dates. On the other hand, he wasn't sure he'd ever cared enough to warn anyone off before.

Rachel's hand settled on his thigh. His attention jerked in her direction.

Her eyes were soft with questions. "What was that about?"

"It was just Jason being Jason." For some reason he didn't want to explain about the bet.

"Why did you tell him we were just old friends?"

"I guess it's a little bit of a stretch." Her lips thinned as she pressed them together. "Why did you give him the impression we're dating?"

"Aren't we?"

"I don't think so." She settled her napkin on her lap. "The term seems too tame for what we're doing."

And wasn't she right about that. He remembered how she'd looked this morning in his robe, the dark blue terrycloth contrasting with her pale skin and matching the midnight blue of her eyes. With her hair soaked from her shower, she'd let him pull her close then shook herself like a dog after a swim. He'd retaliated by dumping her onto the mattress and making her all sweaty again. Then, he'd joined her for her second shower of the morning.

Desire seared him, hot and consuming. He laid his arm across the back of her chair and leaned close. When she glanced his way, he captured her gaze and gave her a glimpse of his hunger. To his intense satisfaction, her lips parted and her cheeks flushed.

With the amount of time they'd spent together in the last week, his body shouldn't be clamoring to ditch the party and take her home, but her touch set off a chain reaction inside him. Two things kept him in place. His mom would kill him if he left, and he was eager to take Rachel in his arms on the dance floor.

He covered her hand with his. Their fingers meshed. His emotions settled. The temperature of his desire dipped from raging boil to slow simmer.

On the opposite side of the table Jason watched him through narrowed eyes. Max knew what his friend was thinking, but he was dead wrong. As Sebastian stood to deliver the first toast, Max let his gaze roam around the tent. All the usual suspects had been invited. Immediate family, extended family and friends. About two hundred people in all. Including his illegitimate half brother, Nathan, who sat two tables over with his very pregnant wife, Emma.

For a moment, Max fought irritation. Nathan's presence shone a spotlight on Brandon's infidelity and made a mockery out of celebrating thirty-five years of marriage. Max had never understood how his mother had allowed her husband to bring Nathan into her home after his mother died. Sure, it was the decent thing to do and his mother was kind and generous, but it had to have killed her to explain to all her friends about the twelve-year-old boy with Brandon's gray eyes. Yet to the best of Max's recollection, he'd never heard a cross word between his parents on the subject. He'd never know if his mother had forgiven her husband, or if she'd just decided to bear the humiliation for the sake of her marriage.

He and Sebastian hadn't followed her example of tolerance toward Brandon and their half brother. Even now, twenty years later, Max couldn't come to peace with his father or Nathan. The anger and resentment bubbled far below the surface like a dormant volcano.

And caught up in all those negative emotions were his feelings for Rachel. He couldn't completely let go of the way she'd deceived him all those years ago. Nor could he turn a blind eye to the secrets he knew she kept from him now.

The secrets that were bound to tear them apart.

"What are you doing out here?"

Max looked up from the steering wheel of the '71 Cuda and spied Rachel standing in the doorway that led from the garage into his back hallway. They'd returned from the party fifteen minutes ago and while she'd disappeared into the bathroom to change clothes and brush her teeth, he'd retreated to the one place in the house that had the most soothing effect on him.

"I'm enjoying my latest purchase."

Rachel stepped into the garage, her three-inch heels giving her long legs a positively sinful appearance. She wore the red and black baby-doll nightie Hailey had packed for the trip to Gulf Shores. That weekend, his appetite hadn't afforded her the chance to wear it. He recalled her opinion about the futility of wearing the thing. That he would have it off her in ten seconds.

"Wouldn't you enjoy it more if you took it for a drive?" She stopped near the front of the car and bent down to slide her palms up the hood. The black lace edging her neckline gaped, baring her round breasts. Beneath his intent regard, her nipples puckered against the gown's thin fabric.

The combination of muscle car and half-dressed Rachel was irresistible. He was instantly hard.

"Feel like going for a ride?" He got out of the car and prowled toward her.

She plucked a condom from inside her bodice and held it up. "Maybe later."

He put his arms around her, hands riding the sexy curve of her butt to the nightgown's hem. "How about now?"

He loved the flow of the material over her warm curves and the contrast between the scratchy lace and her silky skin. But he adored the heat between her thighs even more. And the low moan of longing that rumbled through her as he dipped his fingers into the moisture awaiting him there.

She pressed hot kisses to his neck as her fingers dipped inside the elastic waistband of his underwear and slid them down his thighs. He kicked free of the material, groaning his appreciation as her hands rolled the condom on his hot shaft.

Her mouth was open and awaiting his kiss as he lifted her off her feet, savoring the damp slide of her hot, sweet center against his belly. Gently, he placed her on the car's hood, past caring what damage he might do to the very expensive collectible. He only gave himself a second to enjoy the sight of

Rachel splayed across the yellow hood, but the mental snapshot was unforgettable.

The elastic band kept the bodice snug against her chest and allowed the rest of the material to billow around the top of her thighs. However, the nightie was so short that when he'd set her on the car, the fabric rode up, exposing her concave belly and the thatch of dark blond curls at the juncture of her thighs. Nothing looked as gorgeous as she did at the moment.

He stepped between her legs and gathered her butt in his hands. Fastening his mouth on her, barely hearing her gasp past the roar in his ears, he feasted on her. She tasted incredible. Mewling sounds erupted from her parted lips as her fingers clutched his shoulders. He laved her with his tongue, penetrating deep while she writhed within his grasp. He drove her toward orgasm without mercy, ignoring her incomprehensible protests. Maybe later he would give her a turn at him. Right now, he wanted to put his mark on her body and soul.

When she was close to the edge, he slipped two fingers inside her and watched her explode. She screamed his name. Her nails bit into his shoulders as her back arched and her heels found purchase on the bumper. Shudder after shudder pummeled her body, wringing every single sensation possible out of her. Only when she went completely limp did he cease his erotic assault and kiss his way up her body.

Sliding his hands under the elastic beneath her breasts, he rode the material up over her head. She blinked and stared at him, dazzled.

"No fair," she complained. "I was going to do that for you."

"Later," he promised, riding the curve of her breast with his lips.

"It'll have to be much later," she agreed, sifting her fingers though his hair. "Because I can't move at the moment."

"That's okay. You just lie back and let me do all the work." He opened his mouth over her nipple, swirling his tongue around and flicking it over the sensitive tip. Her body jerked as he grazed his teeth against her flesh.

"Whatever you say." She closed her eyes. A half smile curved her lips. She looked the picture of utter contentment.

His heart turned over. It was happening to him all over again. He was falling beneath her spell. Her palms glided along his biceps as he nudged against her entrance. She was so slick, he almost drove straight in. But a week of intense lovemaking had taken the sharp edge off his driving need. He intended to savor every inch of their joining. To take his time enjoying the tight sheath that seemed made just for him.

And to watch her expression as he did so.

For it seemed the only time she truly dropped her guard and let him in was when he was buried inside her. That's when she couldn't fight what she needed or hide her thoughts.

He eased forward, delighting in the play of happy emotions across her features. When he was fully embedded, she surrendered a smile of sheer delight and opened her eyes. Plummeting into their blue depth, Max sank past her doubts and fears to her true heart. Jewel bright, her joy welcomed him. Pure and fierce it connected him to her.

"Again," she coaxed, cradling his face between her hands. "I love the feel of you sliding inside me."

He was happy to oblige her. She crooned her delight as he completed another long slow thrust. It was then that she wrapped her legs around his hips and began moving with him. He increased his rhythm. Pleasure built in slow waves as he took his time and gave her more of exactly what she liked.

And when he came, the pressure, swelling low in his back, exploded through him like a concussion bomb. The waves of pleasure caught Rachel and pulled her into bliss along with him. He lowered his head and touched his lips to hers, fusing their mouths together in a kiss of tender passion.

"Best ride of my life," he murmured against her neck as his heart labored and his lungs pumped.

Her nails grazed along his back to the base of his spine. "Better than racing around the track at a hundred twenty miles an hour?"

"Much, much better."

With his body mostly recovered, he gathered her in his arms and carried her back to bed. Once there, she snuggled at his side, her head on his shoulder, hand on his chest. Peace swept over him. He liked falling asleep next to this woman. Sleepovers were something he usually frowned on. They suggested a level of intimacy he avoided with all the women he dated.

Rachel was different. She knew they had no future. Only the present. They weren't dating. They were lovers. Lovers without expectations. She understood and accepted the limits of their relationship.

Because after much soul-searching tonight, he'd decided it was all he could offer her.

Nine

Max finished interviewing the last of the candidates Rachel had sent him. His respect for her ability to match employer to employee had increased over the last two days. She'd even scheduled the four women in order of their compatibility for both him and the type of work he would have them do, starting with the most likely candidate first and finishing with the woman he liked least.

They were all beautiful. Single. Intelligent. A month ago, fantasizing about any one of them could have occupied him for hours.

Today, his thoughts centered around one woman. Rachel. With her wise and witty opinions of the four candidates melding with his impression of them, he couldn't help but appreciate their similar thought patterns. Already he missed her sitting outside his door. He hadn't realized how often he'd walked past her desk so that he could deliver a remark guaranteed to make her grin or frown at him.

"Thank you for coming by on such short notice," he told the last candidate as he handed her off to his temporary assistant. A capable woman in her fifties, she'd been sent by Rachel to fill in for a few days. "Cordelia, can you show her out?" To his chagrin, he'd already forgotten the candidate's name.

"Of course." Cordelia stood. "And there's a young woman waiting for you in the lobby. Hailey Lansing."

Curious why Rachel's sister would have come to see him, Max headed for the lobby.

"Hailey?" He approached her with a smile. "To what do I owe the honor of your visit?"

Rachel's sister rose to her feet and took the hand he extended. Her brows darted together. "Thanks for seeing me like this. I probably should have called."

Something about Hailey's grave expression and obvious agitation put Max's instincts on red alert. Here was his chance to find out what was really going on with Rachel. She might never forgive him for going behind her back, but if he had to lose her, at least he could say that he'd done everything he could to straighten out whatever had gone wrong in her life.

"Let's get out of here." He gestured toward the elevator. Whatever Hailey had to say involved her sister and he thought it might go down easier with a single-malt scotch.

As the elevator door closed on them, Hailey twisted her engagement ring around and around on her finger and shot him an uncomfortable half smile. "You're probably wondering why I came to see you."

"You could say that."

Given Rachel's proclivity for keeping her problems hidden from everyone in her life, he was dying to know what had brought Hailey to his doorstep. And why she was wringing her purse strap like a dishcloth.

He escorted her across the lobby to the restaurant that occupied a large chunk of the first floor. Known for its fabulous cuisine and rich ambiance, it was a favorite place for those in the surrounding buildings to bring clients. It was also packed for happy hour, but at three in the afternoon, it was early enough that Max was able to find them a table in a quiet corner of the bar.

The waiter brought his usual and Hailey surprised him by ordering a martini.

At his expression, she offered him a weak smile. "It's been a long week."

Even though it was only Wednesday, Max agreed. "What can I help you with?"

"My sister."

Of course. "I thought that might be why you came by." He let an ironic smile kick up one side of his lips. "She's no longer working for me directly."

"I know."

"Then, I'm not sure what I can help you with."

The waiter placed their drinks before them. Hailey took a long sip of her martini before answering. "I found out from our neighbor last night that someone slashed Rachel's car tires."

Max stared into the amber depths of his drink. "Yes, I know. It happened sometime between Friday night when I picked her up and Sunday evening when I dropped her off."

"I knew it." Hailey flashed her straight, white teeth in a triumphant grin.

"Knew what?"

"That you two were involved. The sexual tension between you that night at dinner was hot."

Max leaned back and redirected the conversation where he wanted it. "Rachel said the neighborhood kids slashed her tires."

"That's what she told me, too, but I know better." Hailey's hunched shoulders suggested she was worried.

Alarm sizzled along his nerve endings. "Then who do you think is responsible?"

"Her stupid ex."

"I didn't realize he lived in Houston." Why hadn't Rachel told him? Why did he even bother asking? She held secrets tighter than a cold-war spy.

"As far as I know, Brody still lives in Biloxi. And my sister doesn't like admitting past mistakes. Brody was a big one."

"Why is that?"

"Because he was a complete jerk. You'd never know it to look at him. He dresses like he's harmless and he can turn that boyish charm of his on and off like a faucet, but beneath the surface, he's creepy."

Something beyond sisterly loyalty tightened Hailey's expression into a stiff mask. Seemed she had a few secrets of her own. But it was the fear that Max glimpsed in her eyes that pumped him full of adrenaline.

"You're not as good at hiding things as your sister. Tell me why he was a complete jerk."

"I didn't spend much time around him, just my last year of high school. And even then, I was cheerleading and on the yearbook staff so I wasn't home much." She took a deep breath and continued. "I didn't like the way he treated Rachel when I wasn't around."

"How did you know how he treated her if you weren't there?"

"Sometimes they didn't know I was home. I spent a lot of time in my room with the door closed. Brody was always on her about putting me first. He said that he was her husband and she should make his needs her priority. I'm ashamed to admit that I was really glad to head off to college. And once I was gone, I stayed away as much as I could, taking summer courses and working." Her chin sank toward her chest. "Part of me hated to leave Rachel alone in that house, but I knew if I showed her I could take care of myself, she could concentrate on her marriage."

"So, he was abusive."

"Not physically. He was too much of a coward to go after her. But I heard them fighting a couple times." Hailey's expression hardened. "Nothing Rachel couldn't handle. My sister's tough. But that's no way to live."

Max acknowledged that with a weary exhalation. "I agree." He didn't like the picture developing in his head. And it made him rethink how angry he'd been with her all those years ago for going back to her ex-husband.

"I guess it's wrong of me to say bad things about him when he paid for my education and everything. That's why I've been paying him back a little every year. I don't want to feel indebted to him at all."

"How much have you paid him?"

"Not much. About twenty thousand."

Max whistled. "That's a pretty big chunk for someone just out of school."

"I still owe him almost eighty." Hailey drew circles around the rim of her martini glass with her finger. "I wish I had it so I could be done with the guy."

"Why did you agree to pay him anything?"

"When Rachel asked him for a divorce he made it pretty clear that he wasn't going to let her go." Hailey winced. "He agreed to let her have a divorce if I paid him back the money he'd shelled out for college."

"That's blackmail."

"It was the only way he'd let her go without a major battle."

Max was liking Rachel's ex-husband less and less with each bombshell Hailey dropped. How had Rachel fallen for a guy like that? Granted, she'd been young, and probably a bit desperate, but had she mistaken gratitude for love? Or was he only hoping that her feelings for such worthless scum hadn't run deep?

"Let me lend you the money to pay off Rachel's ex-husband."

Hailey looked appalled. "That's not why I wanted to talk to you. What you must think of me."

She looked ready to walk out on him. Max put a hand on her arm to calm her. The sisters were very much alike. He hoped her fiancé had a clue what he was getting into. "I think you're charming. And crazy to repay someone like your ex-brother-in-law."

Her features settled into a mutinous expression she'd learned from her sister. "I pay my debts."

"Of course you do," he soothed. "And that's why I offered you the loan. Rachel's ex sounds unstable. I would just feel better if he was out of both of your lives for good."

Hailey shook her head. "Forget about me. It's not me he's harassing. Would you be willing to help Rachel in the same way?"

"Of course." He was insulted she even needed to ask. "But she won't tell me what's wrong much less accept my help. In fact, we had a big fight about it."

"But enough to break up over?"

"No." But it was why he feared their relationship might be over. Pain stabbed his chest. "Why do you ask?"

"Because she's been moping around lately like you two were done." The look she leveled at him was fierce and concerned. "I hope you mean to stick around. The last time you walked away she was different."

"I didn't walk away. She did. She got in a car with her ex-husband. She left me." Was he going to let her walk away from him again? The decision to fight for her had been gaining momentum in his subconscious. He might have noticed sooner if he'd stopped behaving like a pigheaded idiot. "Why did you assume I left her?"

"When we met, I recognized you from a picture she kept on her computer of the two of you. She hadn't looked that happy since before Dad died. I couldn't imagine her giving that up." Hailey's voice trailed away. She looked rattled.

As rattled as Max felt. Those days with Rachel had been the best moments of his life. But Rachel had gone back to her husband. And now he was back in her life again.

Max couldn't lose her this time. "How can I help?"

"She borrowed money from Brody to start the business. He showed up a couple weeks ago to collect the full amount. She paid him, but I don't think she had enough to pay him all of it."

"Is that why he's harassing her? How much is left to pay?"

"I think around twenty-five thousand."

Peanuts. Such a small amount shouldn't cause this much drama.

"Are you sure Brody's hanging around because of the money she owes him?"

"Why else?"

"Maybe he wants her back. You said he was possessive and gave her a hard time about the divorce. So much that you two left town to escape him. If he tracked her down after five years only to call for the money she owes him, why hasn't he come after you, too?"

Hailey's eyes widened. "Do you think he might come after me?"

He hadn't meant to upset her further. "Not if he hasn't already. No. I think this is personal." And if it was, Max was going to make sure Brody stayed out of Rachel's life for good. "Do you have a phone number for this guy?"

"I took it off Rachel's cell."

"Give it to me. I'll take care of him."

Ten

Rachel's office phone rang and her stomach dropped. Ten days had gone by since she'd gone with Max to his parents' anniversary party. Two days ago Max had hired his new assistant. She hadn't heard from him once since. Had her contact with him started and ended with his employment needs? If so, what had the amazing sex on Saturday night been about? Good-bye?

Hearing the phone ring had become torture. Any call could be Max. How should she act with him? Professional? Friendly? What should she say? Were they moving to a different level?

But he never called and she wasn't sure where they stood.

Nevertheless, every time she picked up the phone, her heart lurched as if it was trying to escape her chest.

"Rachel Lansing."

"Well, if it isn't my beautiful girl."

Rachel shuddered. Brody had always called her that and

never meant it. She'd never been his idea of beautiful. Just his idea of someone he could manipulate.

"What do you want, Brody?"

"I want you to meet me."

She rolled the phone cord around her finger. "Why? I already told you I can't pay you anything. There's no need for us to meet."

"The guy I owe money to isn't going to give up unless you tell him that."

"Why do I need to tell him anything? And what makes you think he's going to believe me any more than he believed you?"

"He just wants to meet you."

Rachel didn't like this one bit. "It has to be somewhere public." With lots of security guards within earshot.

"How about that place in the lobby where your boyfriend works? We could have drinks. Catch up."

"He's not my boyfriend." The restaurant in the lobby of Max's building? "Not there. Choose some other place."

"Can't. I already told the guy we'd meet in the bar. Be there at three."

He hung up. Rachel stared at the phone in her hand, consumed by the urge to slam it repeatedly on the edge of her desk. Acid burned her stomach. What was going on? Had Brody told the guys about her connection to Max? Would they follow him to his car one night and slash more than his tires?

Rachel wanted to scream in frustration. She couldn't let anything happen to Max. If that meant meeting Brody and the thug he owed money to, so be it.

Exactly at three, she pushed through the lobby doors and headed toward her rendezvous with Brody and his loan shark. For about the hundredth time she wondered what the hell she was doing. These were dangerous men. But it was a public place. And if it got her off the hook then it would be worth her trouble.

She spotted Brody before she reached the restaurant. He was deep in conversation with another man who faced away from her. She'd recognize those broad shoulders and the arrogant stance anywhere. Max. Her heart hit her toes as the worst of her imagined scenarios began to play out.

Max handed Brody a thick envelope and slid a folded piece of paper into an inner pocket of his suit coat before heading toward the elevator without ever noticing her standing in stunned immobility in the middle of the enormous lobby.

Brody spotted her as soon as Max headed for the elevator. A broad smirk transformed his boyish good looks into engaging handsomeness. The effect was lost on Rachel. She stalked over to him.

"What were you doing with Max?" She pitched her voice low, conscious that Max stood twenty feet away waiting for the elevator.

Brody waggled the envelope. "Collecting the money you owe me."

"Give me that." She made a swipe at the envelope, but Brody lifted it out of her reach.

"I don't think so."

"That money doesn't belong to you."

"The hell it doesn't." Brody's smug smile made her grind her teeth.

"Where's the guy who's been threatening me?"

Brody laughed. "You're such a sap. There never was anyone. I knew you needed motivating so I made him up."

"No guy?" She shook her head, confused. "But you owe someone the money?"

"Nope. I needed the fifty grand to buy into this poker game a buddy of mine is running. I knew you wouldn't give me the money unless you thought I needed help. I remember how scared you were when I owed money to Chuckie back when we were married."

"Poker?" Was she that much of a sucker? Shame overrode her other emotions for a moment. Then she grasped what Brody had done. "You terrorized me and my sister over a stupid poker game?"

Rachel saw red. She raised her fists, ready to beat him silly, but spotted Max returning across the lobby toward them. Her hands fell to her sides, the fight draining out of her.

Max stepped between her and Brody. "Get out of here," He addressed the command to her ex. "And don't let me catch you anywhere near Rachel or her sister ever again."

He might be a bully with her, but Max's threat made him pale. However, when Max made no further move against him, Brody sneered at Rachel and departed across the lobby toward the street.

Frustration surged as Rachel watched her ex-husband getting away. "Damn it, Max." She turned the full brunt of her irritation on him. "What the hell did you do?"

"I paid your debt with your ex. You don't have to worry about the guy ever showing up again."

Dismay consumed her. "You paid my debt? I didn't ask you to do that." Now she was in his debt. Someplace she'd sworn never to be.

"Yours and Hailey's. He's out of both of your lives forever."

Rachel stared at him, some of her anger draining away. "Hailey didn't owe him any money."

Max nodded. "She did. She was paying him back for her schooling."

"What?" Rachel struggled to breathe as the weight of these new revelations crushed her.

"It was the only way she could get him to leave you alone. He agreed to stay out of your life if she reimbursed him the hundred thousand for her college education." Max frowned down at her. "Only you had to go and borrow money to start your agency and bring him back in."

She ripped her wrist from his grasp. "I didn't borrow money from him," she snarled. "I told Hailey that so she wouldn't know what was really going on." Bitter laughter tore from her throat. "What a bunch of idiots we all are. I was already paying Brody back for her schooling. It was part of our divorce decree. He played all of us. You. Me. Hailey." She set her back against a nearby pillar as strength left her limbs. "How much did you give him?"

Max didn't look the least bit worried about what she'd just told him. "A hundred and five thousand dollars."

Rachel gaped at him. "What? Why so much?"

"The twenty-five you owed him plus the eighty Hailey still owed."

"How much had she paid him already?" She shut her eyes, fought tears, and awaited the answer.

"Twenty."

Helpless fury welled up inside her, but she didn't have the energy to vent it. Hailey had been paying Brody behind Rachel's back? That hurt.

"Rachel?" Concern tempered Max's tone. "What the hell is going on?"

She looked up at him. His brows had come together in a concerned frown that made her stomach turn cartwheels. From deep inside her mind, Devon's words surfaced.

Or maybe he's found the one he wants.

Her heart ached for it to be true, but Rachel shied away from the foolish hope.

"I need to get out of here," she said. "I need to find Brody and get that money back."

Max caught her arm. "I don't want you anywhere near him."

"I can't owe you."

"You don't."

"I do. You paid my debt."

"To get him out of your life, forever. If you hadn't shown up today you'd never have known about our deal." Max's steel gray eyes sliced at her. "Isn't that the way you work? Keeping everyone in your life in the dark about what's going on with you."

"That's not fair. I was only trying to protect Hailey."

"Fair? Do you think it was fair of you to keep the truth from your sister? She was paying your ex-husband a hundred thousand dollars to protect you."

Rachel gasped. "She didn't need to do that. I had everything all worked out."

"Only she didn't know that, did she? You were too busy keeping her wrapped in cotton to realize that by isolating her, you made her vulnerable."

"I was trying to keep her safe."

"And she was trying to help you. But you couldn't let her. You can't accept help from anyone."

Max's accusations lashed at her. Unable to deny that they made sense, she retreated into her convictions. What he said rang true, but it was only half the story.

"For good reason."

"Care to share?"

She recoiled. Telling Max about the mistakes she'd made with Brody would substantiate every negative thought he'd ever had about her. Rachel wasn't convinced she was strong enough to watch his concern die, but what choice did she have?

"So you agreed to pay him for Hailey's education."

"I didn't borrow money from Brody to start up the business. I was paying him so he would agree to a divorce."

"How much?"

"A hundred thousand dollars."

"Why so much?"

"That's how much it cost to put Hailey through college."
All at once, the secrets she'd lived with for years could no
longer be contained. "Brody used me to keep his gambling a
secret from his father. While I was married to him, he put me
on the payroll for more than what I should have been earning. I was supposed to use the money for Hailey's school, but
most of the time, there wasn't enough because he was losing
the money playing poker. To get what I needed, I waitressed
on the weekends he was gone."

"He was stealing money from the company."

"I guess."

"How much of Hailey's education did you pay for by wait-
ressing?"

"By the end, I was paying for all of it." She circled her
hand in a vague gesture. "That's when I wanted out. But
Brody hired the best divorce attorney in Biloxi and contested
everything. I was desperate enough to agree to anything to
get away from him."

"I don't understand why you let him do that to you."

"Because I was young and scared. When I met Brody, I'd
been taking care of Hailey by myself for a year and slipping
a little further behind every month. Our apartment was a
dump. We clipped coupons and barely scraped by. Most days
I didn't see how I was going to make it to the next paycheck.
Then Brody swept into my life. He seemed like a dream come
true. Wealthy, handsome, charming, and he saw me as the
perfect patsy. Stupid and gullible." Rachel turned away from
Max, unable to face her failure reflected in his eyes. "I guess
some things haven't changed. I came here today because he
said that I needed to meet with the guy who slashed my tires
and convince him that I wasn't going to be able to come up

with any more money. Only there wasn't any guy threatening Brody."

"He lured you here to see me giving him the money. He
wanted to hurt you."

He wanted to humiliate her. To demonstrate he'd always
be smarter than her. "How did you know about him? About
the money I owe him?"

"Hailey. She was worried about you and came to me for
help. Did you know she was paying your ex for her tuition?"

"What?" This was a complete disaster. Now she had to
have a long, painful talk with her sister. "Why would she do
that?"

"Brody convinced her the only way he would give you a
divorce is if she paid him back for tuition."

"She did it because we were worried about you. Why can't
you just say thank you for the help?"

Failure buzzed around her head like a swarm of black flies.
She'd screwed up again. Self-loathing flared, setting fire to
her irritation.

"I didn't ask for her help or yours."

"Maybe everything would have turned out better if you
had." Max's gaze warned her to stay silent as she opened her
mouth to disagree. "You brought this whole mess on yourself
and on us because you had to do it all yourself. You couldn't
reach out for help. You couldn't accept assistance when it was
offered. Instead, you alienated Hailey and me and made it so
your ex-husband could cheat both of us."

"You'll get every penny back," she retorted, her face hot
while the rest of her body shivered with chill. "If it takes me
until the day I die, I'll pay you back every cent."

"I don't care about the money. I only care about you." He
reached for her, but Rachel flinched back. It was instinctive
reaction to Max's earlier scolding, but his gray eyes became

like a wintry sky, dense and ominous. "Only you won't let me do that."

And to Rachel's profound dismay, he turned on his heel and walked away from her. She wrapped one arm around her waist and ground the knuckles of her other hand against her lips to keep from calling him back. The set of his shoulders told her he was completely done with her.

As he should be.

He was right. This was all her fault. She'd made nothing but one mistake after another since the day her father died. She'd trusted the wrong people. She'd allowed fear to make her weak. And when she learned to be strong, she swung so far in the other direction that she'd put up walls that kept out even the people she loved.

She didn't blame Max for walking away. In fact, she was a little surprised he hadn't run as far and fast as he could to get away from her. She owed him more than she could repay. Not just the money he'd given Brody, but for stepping in on her behalf as well as on Hailey's.

What a fool she was to have shut him out. She was an even bigger fool to let fear of rejection stand in the way of her chasing after him now.

Max went straight to the parking garage. His footfalls ricocheted around the concrete structure, mimicking the echo in his empty chest. He'd called his new assistant and warned her he'd be gone the rest of the day. Taking off in the middle of the afternoon wasn't like him, but what was the point in trying to work when there was no way he could concentrate?

He eased his car up the exit ramp and rolled down the window to activate the garage's electronic gate. Heavy, humid air, stinking of exhaust, washed over him as his tires reached the street. He longed for the clean scent of the beach. But even that wouldn't soothe him for long. The fragrance would forever remind him of Rachel and their time together.

How could two people be so right for each other and so wrong at the same time?

The question made him think of his parents' past troubles, and before he knew his intention, the car was heading to the suburbs. He called ahead to make sure someone was home and his mother met him at the door.

"Your father is golfing," she said, drawing him through the house with her arm linked through his. "He appreciates playing so much more now that he's back to work part-time. I've never seen him so relaxed. He'll be back in an hour or so if you can wait around that long."

"I didn't come about business. I need to talk to you."

"Really?" Her surprise faded to concern as she scanned his face. "Is it something serious? You're not ill, are you? You look awfully pale. Are you sleeping?"

"Nothing like that." Max patted her hand to reassure her. "It's about Dad's affair." Max felt his mother's whole body stiffen. He kicked himself for being so blunt. "If it's too hard for you to talk about, I'll understand."

"No." The word swept out of her on a gust of air. "It's okay. I should be able to talk about it after twenty years, right?"

"It's okay if you can't."

She didn't speak until they'd entered the kitchen and she'd pushed him onto a stool at the breakfast bar. In his childhood home, the kitchen had been separate from the rest of the house, a place where the housekeeper prepared meals and he and Sebastian snuck snacks. In this house, the kitchen opened onto a large great room with overstuffed couches and an enormous flat-screen television. A sunroom had been transformed into a semiformal dining area for eight and a breakfast nook held a table that seated four.

Although the house possessed a formal dining room designed to entertain on a grand scale, the room was used infrequently. For holidays, birthdays and spontaneous dinners, the family gathered in this casual space.

From the refrigerator, his mother brought out white cheddar cheese, pâté, and olives. From the pantry, two types of crackers. By the time she handed Max a glass of crisp chardonnay, an empty plate and a napkin, he was grinning.

"What's so funny?" she demanded, handing him a cracker spread with pâté.

"I didn't realize it was happy hour."

"It's five o'clock somewhere." She waved her hand at him and sipped her own wine. "I tried a new recipe for the pâté. I'd like your opinion, but only if you rave about my wonderful cooking. Now, what did you want to know about your father's relationship with Marissa?"

Nathan's mother's name slipped off her tongue with ease as if she'd spoken it a thousand times.

"It really isn't the affair I'm interested in. I wanted to know why you forgave Dad after what he'd done to you." Max popped the cracker into his mouth and chewed. "Or maybe I should ask how you forgave him."

"I loved him."

"That's all there was to it?" Max couldn't shake his disappointment. He wanted a concrete, step-by-step plan that he could apply to his own difficulties with Rachel. "You didn't weigh your options then decide do it to keep the family together or because he promised never to do anything like that again?"

His mother shook her head. "No. I forgave your father for purely selfish reasons. I didn't want to live without him."

"Even knowing he hadn't been honest with you?" The question struck at the heart of what he couldn't grasp. "What assurance did you have that he wouldn't lie again?"

"None." His mother cocked her head. "I went on faith."

"That's it?" Damn it. The answer to such a complex problem couldn't be that simple. "After everything that happened you didn't want a guarantee?"

"What assurance do you have that someone will love you forever or that they ever intended to keep vows they made? 'Til death do us part. How many people believe in that anymore? The vows should say, ''til we're no longer willing to work on our marriage.'"

His mother's pragmatism left Max momentarily speechless.

"But you and Dad just renewed your vows. Why did you do that if you didn't believe in them?"

"Did I say I didn't believe in them? I took my vows to your father very seriously." She handed him a slice of cheese. "And just so you know, it was his idea to renew our vows. It's taken us a lot of work to get to where we are today. But I can say with confidence that your father and I are more in love and more committed to each other than we were the day we got married."

Max chewed on the cracker and pondered his mother's words.

He loved Rachel. There was no sense in denying it any longer. Her stubborn need to reject all outside help had given him the excuse he needed to hide from the truth in his heart. No matter how many secrets she kept from him, she wasn't deceitful because she was a bad person. She merely struggled to trust anyone. And after what she'd been through, could he blame her? He had his own issues with trust.

"Is this about that woman you brought to the party?" his mother asked, stepping into the silence. "I liked her very much." Her lips curved in a wry grin. "I got the distinct impression you did, as well. You two left here early enough."

Max felt a little like a teenager caught in the backseat of

the car with a half-naked girl. "We've been seeing each other for a few weeks."

"And she's important to you."

"Yes."

"But there's a problem of trust between you?"

"We met five years ago. She was married at the time, although I didn't find that out until after we…" He paused, groping for a delicate way to put it.

His mother played with her diamond tennis bracelet. "Spent some time together naked?" While he regarded her in dismay, she chuckled. "Oh, I wish you could see the look on your face right now."

Max dove back into the story. "I was so angry when I found out. With everything that happened with Dad you know I wouldn't have gotten involved with her if I'd known." Or would he? The chemistry between them had been hot and all consuming. Would he have walked away if she'd told him up front that she was in an unhappy marriage?

"She's divorced now, I take it."

"For four years. When we met, she didn't tell me she was married. I found out when her husband showed up to bring her home."

"And you overreacted because you've always taken issue with your father for cheating on me. If you love her, you can't continue to punish her for mistakes she made."

"I don't want to punish her." But wasn't his inability to trust her just as detrimental to their relationship?

"If you can't forgive her, you might have to give up and let her go."

But his mother hadn't given up and Max needed to know why. "Why didn't you leave?"

"Some things are worth fighting for. Your father was one of them."

"Even after he'd lied to you and had an affair?"

"Not just an affair," she told him, her voice and eyes steady. "He loved Marissa. I don't know why he never left me for her."

Max's temper simmered at the old hurts. "You didn't ask?"

"It was enough that he stayed."

He remembered those days. His mother had been depressed and on the verge of tears much of the time. Max hadn't understood what was happening between his parents until Nathan appeared, but he'd been mad as hell at his dad for upsetting his mom.

Max still didn't understand his mother's ability to forgive his father. Sure, she loved him and wanted to keep her family together, but she wasn't bitter or angry about the past. It was as if she understood she needed to let it go in order to be happy in the future.

"And he promised it would never happen again," his mother continued.

"You believed him?"

"Yes." She lifted her hand and showed off the five carat diamond ring Brandon had bought to renew their vows. "And we're still married because I did."

"I'm not sure I have it in me to forgive Dad."

"I wish you would. Hanging on to the past isn't healthy. You've let what happened between your father and me keep you from falling in love and getting married. Rachel seemed like a lovely woman. I can't imagine that you would care for her if she wasn't wonderful. Forgive them both. I think you'll find doing so will set you free."

"I'll think about it," Max muttered, but even as he said the words, he felt himself resist.

Rachel hadn't wanted to interrupt Hailey at work, but she desperately needed to talk to her sister. She called Hailey and invited her to dinner. Then, she went to the grocery store and bought what she needed to make their father's famous pan-fried grouper.

The domestic routine soothed her. She'd been rushing around so much these last few weeks, between her business and Max's office, fitting in a couple hours to cook and eat a meal hadn't been a priority.

It was time she slowed down.

By six o'clock when Hailey arrived, Rachel had made a mess of the kitchen but had fun doing it.

"Whoa. What's with this? You're cooking?" Hailey dropped her purse on the small breakfast table and surveyed the mess Rachel had made. She wrinkled her nose at the spilled flour, puddles of buttermilk and the array of spices and bowls that occupied every square inch of countertop. "Now I remember why I took over cooking. You are a disaster in the neatness department."

"Don't I always clean up when I'm done? Get changed and come open a bottle of wine."

"I'll be right back."

Only a twinge of guilt pinched Rachel as she directed her sister to the bottle in the refrigerator.

Hailey pulled it out and peered at the label. "Champagne? What are we celebrating?"

"I had some good news today."

"A new client?" Hailey worked off the foil and pried at the cork.

"Better." Rachel waited until her sister was fully engaged in wiggling the cork free before she unloaded her bombshell. "Max paid off Brody."

The bottle jerked. The cork shot out with a loud pop and dented the ceiling. Hailey stared at Rachel with her mouth open as foam flowed down the side of the bottle onto the floor.

"He did?"

"Any idea how Max found out that Brody was hassling me about money?"

"I told him." Hailey looked one part anxious and one part resolute. "Are you mad?"

Damn right she was mad. But confronting Hailey about seeking Max's help wasn't satisfying. Tension flowed out of her, leaving behind nothing. Not even regret.

"No. I'm angry with myself. I should have told you the truth instead of trying to protect you." Rachel's eyes burned as she reached into the cupboard and brought out two water glasses. The only pair of champagne glasses she'd ever owned had been bought for her wedding toast. She'd smashed them not long after her first anniversary.

Hailey poured the champagne. "I wish you had. It would have made things a lot easier for both of us."

"Here's to honesty between sisters from here on out." Rachel clinked her glass against Hailey's.

"I'll drink to that," Hailey said. "Tell me what happened today."

"Why don't you start by telling me what possessed you to go to Max."

Hailey shot her an accusing look over the rim of her glass. "You are mad."

"I'm not," she started, but her sister's impatient huff reminded her of their toast. "Okay, I'm not exactly mad at you. I get why you did it. I just wish you hadn't."

"I had to. Someone slashed your tires. That scared me."

Rachel flinched. "I had it under control."

"No, you didn't." Hailey's voice was hot as she countered Rachel's claim. "Just like you didn't have it under control after Dad died and Aunt Jesse took off on us. I know I wasn't out of high school, but you should have let me help."

"I was trying to protect you."

Hailey shook her head. "You always treated me like I was

made of glass. Just once I wanted you to lean on me, but you never did."

"I didn't realize it was that important to you," Rachel said, holding up her hands to fend off her sister's verbal battery. She'd always been proud of her sister, but never more than now. "Thank you for going to Max."

Hailey's temper evaporated. Her lips formed a half grin. "Wow, how'd that taste?"

"Bitter." Rachel finished the rest of her champagne in one swallow and held her glass out for a refill. "If you hadn't gone to him, Brody would have continued to pester us. He'd have taken more of your money. And I would forever be hopeful that Max might someday forgive me for not telling him I was married five years ago. I don't need to worry on any of those accounts any more."

"You and Max will make it work. That man has it bad for you."

"You didn't see him today. He never wants to see me again. Thanks to me he paid a hundred and five thousand dollars to a lowdown stinking liar."

"Why so much? You only owed him twenty-five."

"But you told Max that you'd promised to pay Brody for your college education."

Hailey gasped. "He wasn't supposed to do that."

"Now do you understand why I kept this from Max?" She slid the cooked fish onto two plates and dished out the broccoli she'd steamed. "He's not the sort of man to stand on the sidelines when he could save the day." Another reason why she loved him. Rachel blew out a breath. "He settled both our debts. I told him I'd pay him back the money. The problem is, you and I were both paying Brody off for your schooling. He was double dipping."

"I thought you were paying him back for a loan to start your business."

"No. Brody was cheating us. We paid him for your schooling twice."

"Twice?" Hailey looked horrified.

"I was paying him as part of our divorce decree. Now paying back Max will make it three times."

"That's insane. You're not going to do that. I'm not going to let you."

Rachel shoved a plate into her sister's hands. "Yes, I am."

"No, you're not. It was my mistake. I'm going to pay Max back."

"It was my fault for not telling you about my arrangement with Brody from the beginning. I'll pay Max back. You're getting ready to start your life with Leo. You don't want this sort of debt hanging over your head."

"And you've got a business to run. You shouldn't have to shoulder it, either."

Rachel had never seen her sister look so fierce or so determined. New respect bloomed. While she'd struggled with her business and finances, Hailey had become a strong, independent-minded young woman. Rachel was ashamed she hadn't noticed sooner.

"Okay."

Hailey's eyebrows shot up. "What do you mean, okay?"

"You're absolutely right that I don't want to be the one to pay Max back."

"You're going to let me do it?" Hailey nodded in satisfaction.

"Nope. I have a different idea altogether." Rachel rubbed her hands together and sent an evil grin winging toward her sister.

Hailey cracked a smile. "Anything you'd care to share?"

"Grab some silverware. We'll talk while we eat."

Eleven

Rachel stood on Max's front porch, her finger hovering over the doorbell. Her enthusiasm for the plan she talked over with Hailey had faded as she'd driven the twenty minutes to his house. What was she doing here? Max wouldn't want to help her after what had happened earlier today. Even if he answered the door, he'd probably slam it in her face as soon as he spotted her standing here.

Maybe he wasn't home. It was a Thursday night. Didn't he get together with his friends and go clubbing on Thursdays? She should have called. But what if he refused to answer?

She should have waited until Monday and caught him at his office. Of course, he might refuse to see her there, as well.

The door opened while lose-lose scenarios played through her mind like an action movie.

"Are you planning on standing out here all night?" Max asked. He blocked the doorway with his arm and nothing about his hard expression or his tense body language gave her hope. But suddenly Rachel's spirits rose.

"I guess I'll have to if you don't let me in."

His eyebrows rose. "What's the password?"

"You were right."

"That's three words."

She dug deeper. "I'm sorry."

"That's two words." A twitch at the corner of his mouth told her she was getting close.

"Help."

He reached out and dragged her inside. "That's it."

Lowering his head, he captured her mouth in a hard, unyielding kiss that melted away her worries. She wrapped her arms around his neck and kissed him back, giving full rein to her angst and fear of losing him.

He stripped off her shirt and dove his fingers beneath the elastic waistband of her skirt, pushing it down her hips until she stood before him in bra, panties and sneakers. Then, he scooped her into his arms and carried her down the hall to his bedroom.

The long walk gave her time to summon explanations or apologies, but Max's grim expression tied her tongue into knots. Make love to him now. Fight with him later. At least they would make another incredible memory for her to relive after they parted ways for good.

When he set her on her feet beside the bed, she grabbed the hem of his T-shirt and raised it past his flat stomach and powerful chest. He helped her by tearing it over his head. A purr-like sound vibrated her throat as she set her palms against his chest and backed him toward the bed.

Her fingers worked at the button and zipper of his jeans. She needed to taste him. The urgency made her clumsy and she let him rid himself of the rest of his clothes. Once he was naked, she dropped to her knees in front of him and sucked

him into her mouth without finesse or preliminaries. He released a hoarse groan as her tongue circled him, discovering
his texture and the best way to give him pleasure.

Before she brought him all the way to release, he stopped
her and pulled her back to her feet. Placing a hot, sizzling
kiss on her lips, he lifted her and deposited her on her back
in the middle of the mattress. She kicked off her shoes. He
followed her down and as his weight pressed her into the mattress, she ran the sole of her foot along his calf.

His fingers hooked around her underwear, stripping it
down her legs. While he cast it aside, she took off her bra.
The contact between her sensitized nipples and his hard chest
set off a chain reaction of desire.

She lifted her hips toward the hand that teased between her
legs, urging him to touch her with wild gyrations and garbled
pleas. A half sigh, half moan broke from her as he slid his
finger into her wetness and penetrated deep. She shuddered
as he began to stroke her, each movement of his hand driving her further toward fulfillment. But that's not the way she
wanted to go. Her nails bit into his wrist.

"Not like this," she gasped as his teeth grazed her throat.
"Make love to me."

"If you insist."

He moved between her thighs, impaling her with one swift
thrust. Hard and thick, he filled her over and over, the fric-
tion driving her crazy with wanting. Together they climbed.
Higher and faster than ever before. When she came, the sensation rolled over her, wave after wave of intense pleasure.
She floated back to earth in slow motion, the thundering
of her heart keeping time with Max's thrusts as he surged
toward his own climax.

Fascinated, she watched him come. His facial muscles
locked in concentration. His eyes, half-closed, snagged with
hers. He set his mouth against hers and plunged his tongue

deep in a sexy kiss that stole her breath. Then his body drove into hers one last time and spasmed in release.

With her arms wrapped around his shoulders, Rachel held on to him and absorbed his aftershocks. Loving Max like this was easy. They knew exactly how to communicate in bed. She'd lost hope at being able to do so anywhere else.

All too soon, Max pushed away and dropped onto his back beside her. He lay with his forearm across his eyes, his chest rising and falling as his body recovered. Unsure if he would welcome her touch now that their frantic coupling was through, Rachel rolled onto her side and tucked her arm beneath her head.

Five minutes passed before he spoke.

"I'm glad you stopped by." Voice neutral. Expression hidden behind his arm. His mood an enigma.

"Me, too."

As much as she longed to cuddle up beside him and feel the reassuring weight of his arm settle around her, she'd made too many mistakes to hope that he felt tender or affectionate toward her.

"I was hard on you earlier," he continued. "I'm intolerant when I don't agree with someone. It's a bad habit of mine." He shifted his arm off his face and set it above his head. His gaze locked on the ceiling. "Or so my mother tells me."

"You were right to be angry. I screwed up. I should have been more up front with Hailey and with you. If I had, none of this would have happened." She paused. "It's my fault that Hailey gave Brody twenty thousand dollars. It's my fault that you gave him a hundred and five thousand. It's not right that he cheated you and I intend to get that money back."

At last, Max looked at her. The iron in his gray eyes made her wish he hadn't.

"How do you intend to go about that?" he demanded, his hard tone warning her he'd better like her answer.

She drew her knees up and bumped his thigh with them. The grazing contact eased the tension between them. "I'm going Biloxi to ask for it back."

"He went to a great deal of trouble to get the money in the first place," Max said, rolling onto his side so that they faced each other. "Have you considered what you'll do if he won't just give it back?"

She offered him a wan smile. "I was hoping you'd come along. I need your help." She held her breath and waited for some sign that he wasn't going to kick her and her crazy idea to the curb. "Please."

"You're asking me to help you?"

"Yes. I need you. I can't do this alone."

Max's arms snaked around her body, pulling her flush against him. With her thigh trapped between his and her head settled on his shoulder, his lips glanced off her forehead. "I'm glad you finally realized that."

The closer they got to Biloxi, the quieter Rachel became. And it wasn't just that she stopped talking. Her entire body stilled as if by remaining frozen, she could become invisible. Max kept glancing her way as they picked up a rental car at the airport and drove through the city.

He longed to reach out and offer her comfort, but she'd locked herself away and drawn the shutters. His fingers beat a tattoo on the steering wheel. The previous evening's connection had faded with the advent of dawn. She'd stood at the foot of his bed and worried the inside of her lip while he made arrangements for their flight to Biloxi.

"Say the word and we'll get right back on the plane and go home to Houston," Max offered.

In the seat beside him, Rachel started as if he'd jumped out and yelled "boo." Beneath his scrutiny she struggled a long moment before mastering the trace of panic in her dark blue eyes. Seeing her vulnerable for even that short second disturbed Max. She was awash in anxiety and trying like crazy to hide it. He was used to her strength and determination. Is this why she was so scared to ask for help?

"We've come all this way," she said. "We're not going back without that money."

Max nodded. He liked the way she said *we,* including him as part of her team, and appreciated what it had taken her to let him in.

"It's going to be okay. I won't let him hurt you ever again."

"I'm counting on that."

To Max's surprise, she reached out and grabbed his hand.

"Is that why you brought me along?" he teased. "Muscle?"

She stroked up his biceps, wrapping long fingers around his upper arm. "Well, you certainly have enough of them to qualify for that. But that's not why you're here."

"Then why?"

"Because I knew you'd want to come." She glanced his way and encountered his frown. Her elaborate sigh filled the car. "Fine. Because I wanted you to come. You make me feel safe in ways that no one ever has before." She pulled a face. "Happy now?"

"Deliriously."

Rachel's directions brought them into a commercial section of Biloxi. Max parked the car in a visitor's spot in front of Winslow Enterprises. As they entered the front door, he watched her gather courage. By the time they'd arrived at the front desk, her spine was straight and her eyes glinted with determination.

"Hello," he said to the receptionist. "I have an eleven o'clock meeting with Carson Winslow."

Rachel jerked in surprise. He could feel her gaze upon him.

"And your name?"

"Max Case."

While the receptionist spoke into the phone, Rachel grabbed on to Max's arm and drew him toward a seating area. "Why are we meeting with Brody's father?"

"I called him with a business proposition."

"Why?"

"You didn't seriously think Brody was going to just return the money because we asked him to, did you?"

From the expression on her face, she hadn't planned beyond demanding the money back.

Max shook his head. "You told me he's been gambling for years. He used you and the huge salary he paid you to hide his problem from his father. Why do you think he was so reluctant to give you a divorce?"

"Because any financial problems we had he could blame on me." Rachel blinked in dazed disbelief like a prisoner coming out of a dark cell. "What has he been doing since then?"

"I don't imagine he's quit gambling."

"Obviously not if he came to me for the cash he needed to get into a high-stakes poker game."

"Mr. Winslow said he'd be right up," the receptionist said with a polite smile before returning to stuffing envelopes.

"So, what's your plan? You're not going to ask Carson for the money, are you? Brody works hard to keep his father completely in the dark."

"And that will work to our advantage."

She frowned at his cryptic reply, but had no chance to ask for clarification because a thin, gray-haired man in his mid-sixties appeared in the doorway that led to the rest of the building.

"Follow my lead," Max murmured as he stepped forward with his hand extended. "Max Case. Thank you for taking a meeting with me on such short notice."

"Not at all. I was intrigued by your call."

"This is my associate." Max stepped to one side so Rachel came into view.

"Rachel?" Carson's smile faltered. "How are you?"

"I'm wonderful. And you?"

While pleasantries were exchanged between Rachel and her former father-in-law, Max observed the interplay with interest. There was no obvious animosity between the pair. Did that mean Carson had no idea what had transpired in his son's marriage?

"Let's head back to my office," Carson said.

Once inside the spacious corner office, Max wasted no time in getting to the point. "You've probably figured out by now that Rachel was the one who pointed me in the direction of Winslow Enterprises."

"I'll admit it clears up how we came to your attention."

Max smiled. "After doing some research on your company, I was able to determine that it's positioned to break out, but you lack the capital and the skilled management to take you to the next level."

Frustration and resignation tightened Carson's mouth into a grim line. Beside him, Rachel had gone so still, Max wondered if she was holding her breath. He matched her immobility, letting his words penetrate Carson's defenses. From what Max had gathered from his sources in Biloxi, ever since Carson had handed the business operations over to his son, the company was floundering.

Carson was at a crossroads. He needed to decide if he was going to let his son take over and risk the company's future, or sell the business and enjoy his retirement.

"What's going on in here?" an unfriendly voice demanded from the doorway.

Rachel shifted in her seat to confront her ex-husband. Her knees bumped Max's thigh. A tremor passed through her, heightening his determination to give her closure with her ex. By the time Max finished with Brody, the guy wouldn't dare bother Rachel or her sister again.

Carson hit his son with a meaningful look. "Max has come to us with a proposition."

"Is that so." Brody's lip curled. "And what is she doing here?"

Rachel inclined her head, all nervousness mastered. With a half smile, she said, "If it wasn't for me, Max would never have become interested in Winslow Enterprises."

The return of Rachel's confidence eased Max's tension.

"Of course, my brothers are not convinced that your company is large enough for us to pursue. But after we get a look at your books, I'm sure they will be persuaded."

Brody's gaze bounced between his father and Max. Anger melted into uncertainty. "Well, it's not for sale."

"You don't get to make that decision," Carson reminded him, his voice tight with reproof.

"Why not? You've put me in charge, haven't you?" Brody seemed to have forgotten that this family squabble was in front of witnesses.

His father's gaze flicked in Max's direction. "We'll discuss this later. Right now I'm going to take Max on a tour of the facility."

"Let me do it," Brody said.

The tension between father and son tainted the air like exhaust as Brody led the way out of the office. But instead of taking Max and Rachel on the tour his father had suggested, Brody steered them into a conference room and shut the door.

"You've got a lot of nerve showing up here," he snarled.

"*We've* got a lot of nerve?" Rachel began, her fingers curled into claws as if she'd like to rip her ex-husband's eyes out. "You bastard. I want the money you stole from Hailey."

"I don't know what you're talking about."

"She's been paying you for her college."

"So?"

"We agreed as part of our divorce settlement that I would pay you for her education. You had no right to go behind my back and demand money from her, as well."

Brody laughed. "Too bad."

"I want every penny back that she gave you."

"Not going to happen."

"You haven't had time to lose all of it."

"I haven't lost any of it."

"Good. Then you can return the hundred thousand you stole from my sister."

"I didn't steal anything from Hailey or you. She agreed to pay me."

"Because she didn't know I was already paying you."

"And whose fault is that? You were always so determined to keep her in the dark about everything. Our marriage. Her education. You made it so easy for me to tell her anything I wanted and have her believe it."

Max decided it was time to step in. "Return the money."

Brody heard the threat loud and clear. "Or what?"

"Or I'm going to make your father an offer on his business he can't refuse and a team of accountants will show up to do due diligence and your father will learn just how much money you've embezzled from this company over the years."

"I don't know what you're talking about." But Brody's bluff fell flat.

Max snorted in disgust. "I can see why you lose at poker as often as you do," he said. "What do you think is going to happen when your father realizes that you haven't kicked your little problem the way you claim you have?"

"You've been stealing from the company?" Rachel looked almost sorry for her ex-husband.

"More so after you two divorced," Max interjected.

"Have you lost your mind?" Rachel questioned. "After he paid off your gambling debt with the Menks brothers, he swore if you gambled again he would sell the company and cut you off without a cent."

Max chipped in. "Imagine how unhappy he would be to hear that you never had any intention of quitting."

"You have no idea what you're talking about."

"Don't I?" Max couldn't believe the guy thought anyone would believe the words coming out of his mouth. "My brother used to be a professional gambler. When he reached out to his contacts they put him in touch with a number of people you've borrowed money from. Your associates were happy to shed light on your past dealings with them." Max shouldn't have enjoyed twisting the knife as much as he was, but this guy had mistreated Rachel and deserved everything he was getting. "And they've agreed to have a chat with your father if I ask them to."

"You're bluffing." Brody's eyes were blind with panic.

"I don't gamble," Max told him. "That means I never bluff. Every negotiation I go into, I'm holding a royal flush. I never lose."

"Everyone loses sometimes."

"The only one who loses today is you. Get the money."

"I don't have it with me." Brody's tone was close to a whine. Despite the air-conditioned comfort of the room, a bead of sweat trickled down his temple.

"Pity." Max set his hand on the small of Rachel's back and turned her toward the conference-room door.

"Wait."

Max turned the knob and opened the door to reveal Carson Winslow. The older man was frowning.

"I thought Brody was going to take you on a tour."

"He's been telling us how much the company means to

him," Max said. "I didn't realize he was so passionate about the business."

From the way Carson regarded his son, the current owner of Winslow Enterprises hadn't, either. "Well, that's good to know."

"Thank you for your time."

Carson shook his head in confusion. "You're leaving? But we never discussed the reason for your visit."

"I had hoped for a more amiable meeting." Max shook hands with the elder Winslow. "However, Brody made his position clear. He's not interested in doing business with me. I'm sure in time he'll regret making such a rash decision." He hit Rachel's ex with a hard stare.

It took a couple seconds for Brody to understand that Max intended to carry out his threat of informing Carson of his son's gambling. Brody glared at Max.

Seeing the unfriendly exchange, Carson turned on his son. "That wasn't your decision to make."

"Take it easy, Dad." Brody put up his hands. "Max just misunderstood my reservations. If I can have a couple minutes with him in private, I'll explain myself better."

While Rachel and Carson headed for the reception area, Max followed Brody down the hall and into his office, wondering what sort of scheme Rachel's ex would come up with now to save his hide.

To Max's surprise, Brody opened his briefcase and took out an envelope.

He tossed it at Max. "Here it is. A hundred grand. Count it if you want."

Max did. "Looks like it's all here."

"This means we're done. You'll leave me alone?"

"As long as you leave Rachel and Hailey alone, you'll never hear from me again."

"Good."

As he neared the lobby, Max caught Rachel's eye and gave her a tiny nod. Her eyes brightened with unshed tears. His heart turned over in his chest. He wanted nothing more than to wrap her in his arms and hug her hurt away. But with Carson looking on, Max limited himself to a brief smile.

"Did you get Hailey's money back?" she quizzed the instant they emerged into the hot Mississippi afternoon.

He handed her the envelope. "A hundred thousand. Just what you asked for."

She pulled out twenty thousand and gave him back the balance.

"I don't think Brody wants to risk his comfortable little world collapsing around him," he said, watching her face as she held her sister's money.

"I probably could have gotten back all the money you paid him."

Rachel shook her head. "I couldn't spend the rest of my life looking over my shoulder, waiting for him to reappear because he thinks he was cheated out of what's rightfully his." She gave him a sad smile. "You won't be around to protect me forever."

They started their relationship again with the understanding that it was temporary, but it stung hearing her talk about a future without him in it.

"If he's so bad, why did you go back to him after we met?"

"I went back to him because he said he'd tell Hailey why I really married him. I didn't want her to be ashamed of me."

"Sweetheart, she loves you, and she's proud of you. Nothing you did could change that."

"But I couldn't take care of her. She was my responsibility and I was failing."

"You were barely able to take care of yourself." Max wrapped his arm around her shoulders and hugged her. "Cut yourself some slack. You did the best you could. No one could fault you for that."

They hadn't gone more than a mile before Max glanced over and saw Rachel's cheeks were wet with tears. He pulled into the first parking lot he came to and parked the car. The instant he shut off the ignition, she leaned against his shoulder. Max twisted in his seat and drew her into his arms.

"It's going to be okay now," he said. "He'll never bother you again."

Cupping her head, he nuzzled her cheek and absorbed her shudders against his chest. He soothed her with long caresses up and down her back until her breath settled into a steady rhythm.

"I can't believe it's really over." She rested her head on his shoulder for a minute longer, before pushing away and wiping her cheeks. "Take me home."

While Max drove back to the airport, Rachel got on her cell phone and gave Hailey a blow-by-blow of the confrontation with Carson and Brody. He only half listened to her voice. The other half of his attention chewed on his reaction to Rachel asking him to take her home.

He knew she meant home to Houston and her house. But he couldn't shake the bone-deep longing to take her back to a home that they'd make together. What was he thinking? Living together? Marriage? Was he ready to take that step? And with Rachel?

His mind cleared.

Of course with Rachel. He'd loved her since the moment they'd met. He'd been thinking of a future with her. No wonder he'd been so crushed to discover she was already married. That she loved someone else.

And now?

Was he ready to let go of past mistakes and start anew? He was. But first he had to settle a little unfinished business with his father. Max knew he'd never be able to move into the future with the old resentment chained to his ankles like a concrete block. He owed Rachel a fresh start.

As the plane lifted off the ground and low clouds obscured her view of Biloxi, Rachel let her head fall back against the seat. She could have been one of those clouds, as light as she felt at the moment. Today, a chapter of her life had ended. A door closed between past and present. She never had to return to Biloxi or think about Brody ever again.

She glanced at the man beside her. Seeing him in action earlier had made her glad he was on her side. He'd been decisive and intimidating. She'd enjoyed watching him outclass her ex-husband. For the first time in ten years she felt completely free.

"You're smiling," Max said, taking her hand and grazing his lips across her knuckle.

"Savoring the victory."

"I had no idea your divorce had been that contentious."

"My entire marriage was that way. When Brody was losing, he was miserable and made everyone around him the same way."

"No wonder you got out."

"I didn't love him."

Max nodded. "After all you'd been through, I understand why you wouldn't."

"Not in the end." The need to unburden herself was probably going to backfire, but he had seen part of the truth. He might as well know it all. "From the start." She plunged on, needing Max to understand what she'd gone through. "I know it was wrong, but you have to understand how it was. I was afraid. I didn't know how much longer I was going to be able to keep feeding us, much less send Hailey to college. When Brody came along, he seemed nice and wanted to help. I told myself I was in love with him when he proposed, but I think I was so relieved at the idea of having a real home again, I lied to myself and to him. I used him."

"People get married for all sorts of reasons. Not all of them are right." Max's eyes were clear and free of reproach.

"You don't hate me?" Rachel couldn't believe she'd been wrong all along. "I married a man I didn't love because I was scared and wanted financial security. Don't you think that makes me a terrible person?"

"No." Max frowned. "Is that what you've been worried about all this time? That if I knew you'd made a mistake at twenty that it would somehow diminish you in my eyes?"

"You already hated me for not telling you I was married five years ago."

"Hated." He echoed the word and rubbed his eyes. "I never hated you. I said some harsh things when I found out because I was angry. But I never hated you."

"Not even a little?"

When he didn't answer right away, Rachel waited, her breath lodged in her chest. He had something on his mind, an emotion that he needed to distill into words.

"You know my father cheated on my mother."

"Yes."

"It nearly destroyed our family. Mom went through a really tough time when Sebastian and I were kids. I had a hard time watching her be unhappy and not being able to do anything about it. I swore I would never involve myself in any sort of extramarital affair. It's one of the reasons I don't want to marry. I can never cheat on my wife if I don't have one."

Rachel stared at their linked fingers. "I never should have started anything with you."

"Don't say that. This isn't your problem, it's mine. And I'm not sure if I'd known from the start that you were married if I would have been able to walk away."

"Of course you could have. You just said that having an affair was something you swore never to do."

"That's what eats at me. When tested, my convictions failed."

"But they didn't. You didn't know I was married until the end."

"And when I did know, that didn't stop me from wanting you." Max's bitter half smile tore at Rachel's heart.

"So, what are you saying? That if I'd stayed, we could have had a future together." She couldn't help the doubt that crept into her tone. "That's a nice happy ending, Max, but you and I both know that it never would have happened. You would have forever resented me for luring you into something that deep down you didn't want."

"You don't know that."

"I saw your face at your parents' anniversary party. You haven't forgiven your father for what he did to your mother twenty years ago. Those same resentments would have colored our relationship. Every time you look at me you see my infidelity. Just like you see your father's."

She saw the truth in his eyes. It sliced deep into her heart. To conceal the wound, she leaned forward and kissed his cheek.

"I don't want that between us," he said.

"Neither do I." Her throat tightened. "It just is."

Twelve

The conversation on the plane ride home ate at Max long after he dropped Rachel at her house. The lingering kiss she'd given him had tasted like goodbye. Her sad smile, a sign marking a dead end.

Being told that he was an unforgiving bastard had never bothered him before. Only Rachel could make him question what good he was doing himself or anyone else by holding twenty-year-old mistakes against his father.

Restless and unable to face his empty house, he called his dad and found him at the golf course once again. However, when Max arrived, Brandon had just finished the round and was having a drink at the clubhouse before returning home.

"Max," Brandon said, getting up to shake his son's hand. "What brings you here?"

"I wondered if we could talk privately."

"Sure." Brandon excused himself from his friends and led the way to the bar. An Astros game filled the television screen behind the bartender. As soon as Max had ordered a whiskey, Brandon asked, "What's wrong? Problems with your brothers again?"

"Nothing like that."

Despite the fact that Max had recently decided a cease fire in the office was more conducive to productivity, his resentment toward the relationship between Nathan and their father persisted. Brandon had always favored Nathan. And why not? He'd been born to the woman Brandon adored. Unlike his first two sons.

Max wondered if that's what had bothered him all these years. His father had never seemed present when Max and Sebastian were kids. And then Nathan came along and suddenly there were family dinners and vacations. Brandon was around more because he preferred Nathan to his older sons and wanted to spend time with him. At least that's what Max's young mind had decided. He saw now that jealousy had buried that idea in his subconscious and tainted his relationship with his father.

"Your mom told me you came by and asked about my affair with Marissa."

Max and his father had always been blunt with each other. Mostly because Max lacked Sebastian's diplomatic skills or Nathan's charm.

"Your affair hurt her."

"I know," Brandon stared into Max's eyes without flinching. "It's something I'll never be able to make up for, even if I spend the rest of my life trying."

"But she forgave you."

"She's a saint. That's one of the reasons why I love her." Brandon's gaze turned to flint. "And don't for a second think I don't. I was wrong to promise her my fidelity and break that trust, but I loved her when we married and I've loved her every day since. Some days better than others."

For the first time ever, Max saw his father's remorse and the conflict that must have raged in him all those years. He hadn't had a string of affairs. He'd loved two women. One he'd married. The other he'd been unable to give up despite knowing his affair hurt both the women in his life.

"Why is this coming up now?" Brandon asked.

Because he'd hung on to his anger at his father and let the woman he loved walk away. He thought about what his mother had said about him overreacting to Rachel being married. If he'd gone after Rachel and found out the sort of bad situation she was in, he might have convinced her to return with him to Houston. If he'd supported her instead of turning his back in anger, she could have started fresh with him. How much pain could have been avoided if he hadn't been so quick to judge her?

"I'm sorry," he told his father. "I should have followed Mom's example and let go of my anger years ago."

For a long moment, Brandon looked too stunned for speech. "You shouldn't apologize," he said at last, his deep voice scored with regret. "I'm sorry I put you, your brother and my wife through hell." Brandon looked older than he had in the year since his surgery. "I've been waiting a long time for you to stop hating me."

"It took falling in love with a very stubborn woman to make me understand that my anger hasn't done me any good."

"Rachel." Brandon's head bobbed in approval. "I was glad to see you two together at our anniversary party. She brought Missy and Sebastian together, you know. If she hadn't found Missy to be his assistant, I don't know what would have happened to your brother. He's happier than I've ever seen him. We have Rachel to thank for helping make that happen."

And that was it in a nutshell, Max realized. Rachel had helped Sebastian. She'd found him the perfect assistant. The perfect mate. Helping was what she did best. Behind the scenes, often at great personal sacrifice.

His heart expanded as an idea took hold.

It was past time someone did something for her in return.

A new client, Devon had said. He'd sent a text to her phone with an address and suite number, but no contact name. She'd called him back, but he hadn't picked up at work and wasn't answering his cell phone. Not surprising. It was past five o'clock on a Friday night. He had a social life. As did Hailey and pretty much everyone else on the planet.

Everyone except her.

In the two weeks since returning from Biloxi, she'd thrown herself into work. Exhaustion helped her sleep, but nothing prevented the dreams where she chased Max through a maze of long, dark hallways, following the sound of his voice, but never able to catch up to him.

She didn't need a professional to analyze her dreams. As much as she longed to be with him, Max was out of reach.

Stepping out of the humid Houston afternoon into the cool comfort of the building's enormous lobby, Rachel felt the first tingle of excitement in weeks. Landing a client in this building would mean big commissions. This was prime downtown real estate, the sort of place she'd hoped to lease for Lansing Employment Agency.

In fact, six months ago, she'd looked here, but the available space, perfect for her needs, had been snapped up the day after she'd toured. With a gym and a whole host of retail and service providers on the first floor, it was a huge step up from the older building near the edge of downtown that she was in now. Rachel let a wistful sigh escape as she rode the elevator to the eighth floor.

The suite had no identifying name on the outside. Not surprising. She'd passed quite a few unmarked offices on the way. Pushing through the door, she hesitated just inside.

No one occupied the reception desk. The space beyond had an empty feel to it. Granted, it was after the normal workday on a Friday, but she'd expected some sign of life.

"Hello?" She felt uncomfortable searching out her contact in the empty office. "It's Rachel Lansing, I believe we had an appointment."

"Surprise!" Out of two offices burst Hailey and Devon. They threw their arms around each other's shoulders and laughed, enjoying her shock.

"What are you doing here?" she demanded, confusion making her cross.

"I work here," Devon explained. "Come see my new office."

"You quit?" Tears popped into her eyes. She couldn't lose Hailey, Max and Devon in the space of a month.

"No." Devon shook his head, his smile bigger than ever.

Rachel took a deep breath, her hurt easing toward confusion. "I don't understand."

"These are our new offices."

She must have misheard him. "Our new what?"

"Offices," Hailey chimed in, rushing forward to enfold Rachel in an enthusiastic hug. "What do you think?"

"That I've died and heaven is an office suite in the best building in downtown Houston."

A pop came from behind Devon, the distinct sound of a cork leaving a champagne bottle.

"Come see your office," Hailey said.

Rachel resisted her sister's tugging. "This is a great idea," she said. "But I've crunched the numbers a hundred different ways and I can't afford to move in here."

"You can," a deep, masculine voice assured her. Max came

down the hall, carrying four flutes of champagne. "Thanks to your sister."

Seeing him wrenched her heart in six different ways. The days of no communication had been excruciating. She had reached for the phone a hundred times and dialed his number at least a dozen. Loving him and knowing that he could never forgive her was agony.

She turned away from his handsome face and stared at her sister. "Hailey, what does he mean?"

"He means that I took the money I got back from Brody and put it toward your offices."

Rachel's spirits plummeted. "Hailey, no. You shouldn't have done that."

"Don't even go there. You put me through school. You suffered with Brody for five years. Let me do something for you."

"But you're getting married. You should use the money for your wedding or a house."

"I'm marrying a man who understands how amazing my sister is and supports my desire to help her with something she's been working toward for four years."

"In other words," Devon piped up. "Say thank you, Rachel."

"Thank you," Rachel echoed, with the slightest touch of irony. Tears burned her eyes. Emotion tightened her throat. She wrapped her arms around Hailey and hugged her hard. "Thank you," she repeated, unable to speak above a whisper.

"Here," Max handed her a glass of champagne, his eyes glinting with satisfaction. Devon handed Hailey a glass. "To Lansing Employment Agency. May it continue matching executives with assistants for many years to come."

They clinked glasses. Rachel sipped her champagne, and then watched the bubbles to avoid staring at Max. Two weeks and two feet separated them. She felt as giddy as a teenager, and just as awkward.

"I have you to thank for this, as well, don't I?" she asked him.

"I might have made a few inquiries."

She suspected he'd done more than that. She wouldn't be surprised if he'd vouched for her, as well. What prompted him to help her? Heaven knew she'd been nothing but a thorn in his side since reappearing in his life. He'd been eager enough to drop her off after their trip to Biloxi. She'd put every scrap of love she felt for him into that kiss and he'd walked away without a backward glance.

"Thanks." She put her hand on his arm. Lightning shot from her fingertips to her toes, awakening every nerve it passed. "You have no idea what this means to me."

"I think I do."

The room fell away as she got lost in the possibilities swimming in his eyes. He took a half step closer, filling her nostrils with his crisp masculine scent, swamping her with the heat from his body and the pull of his charisma.

"Max, I'm sorry about everything."

He plucked her glass from her numb fingers and set it on the receptionist desk. "You have nothing to be sorry for."

"Brody. The money."

"Gone and returned." His hands slid around her waist, drawing her against him. "I'm the one who's sorry."

"For what?"

"For making you the scapegoat for my problems with my father." He drew his thumb against her cheek. "Being with you, I felt things that made me question what I believed was right. For years I'd been angry with my father for cheating, and with his mistress for refusing to give him up. I resented my mother because she clung to love when self-preservation should have told her to walk away. Wanting you demonstrated that I was no better than them. I was ready to sacrifice my principles to have you in my life."

"But you were so angry when you found out I was married."

"I was angry because you went back to your husband."

"I didn't think I had a choice." And now she understood what a mistake she'd made.

"You put Hailey's needs above your own. How can I be angry about that?"

Rachel snuggled against his chest, hiding her tears from him. For the first time in forever, her life was perfect. She wanted to savor the moment. All too soon, Max pushed her to arm's length. She dabbed at the corners of her eyes with the back of her hand and sniffled.

Glancing around, she realized the offices were empty. "What happened to Hailey and Devon?"

"I think they had someplace else to be."

"Is this really all mine?" She still couldn't believe what Hailey and Max had done for her.

"All yours."

"When I didn't hear from you after getting back from Biloxi, I thought we were done."

"I needed a little time to settle my past where it belonged."

"And now?"

"Put to rest."

As nice as all this sounded, she wasn't sure what happened next. "I'm glad." She pushed aside her doubts about the future and concentrated on enjoying her present. "Can I buy you dinner to celebrate?"

"I have an errand to run, but after that, I'm free."

"How long will it take? Shall I meet you somewhere?"

"Not long. I could use your help, if you don't mind."

"Sure."

They exited the suite, Rachel taking care to lock the door

behind her. The hand Max placed against the small of her
back spread warmth throughout her entire body. Contentment radiated to every nook and cranny, bringing light to
the darkest recesses of her soul.

He gave her an address and directions before they parted
on the downtown street. Still floating in her happy bubble,
she scarcely noticed the rush-hour traffic as she crept toward
the suburbs. By the time she parked in front of an elegant
colonial in one of Houston's older, affluent neighborhoods,
she'd decided whatever form Max wanted their relationship
to take, she'd enjoy being with him as long as he wanted her
around.

While she wondered who lived in the house, Max drove
up past her in a familiar yellow convertible and parked in the
driveway. Her cheeks heated as she recalled what had happened on the hood of that car. Mystified by the reason he was
driving one of his rare cars, she crossed the lawn toward him.

He'd discarded his suit coat and tie and rolled up his
sleeves. She took the hand he held out to her and let him
lead her toward the front door.

"What are we doing here?" she asked as they waited for
the owner to answer their knock.

"You'll see."

His mischievous grin told her he wasn't giving anything
away. A second later, she was distracted by the blond man
who opened the door. Jason Sterling, Max's best friend. His
gaze bounced from Max to her to the car in the driveway.

He paled beneath his tan.

"Oh, man, I never thought I'd see the day." Jason stepped
back to let them enter the house. "Are you sure you want to
do this?"

"Never more sure of anything in the world." He tossed his
keys to Jason and wrapped his arm around Rachel's waist,
guiding her into the foyer.

She gazed up at him, deciding she'd never seen him so relaxed. "Why did you give Jason your car keys?"

"Not just the keys," Jason said.

"The car."

"But you love that car," she exclaimed. "Why would you sell it?"

Max raised his eyebrows. "I didn't sell it."

"I won it."

Rachel regarded the two men for a long moment, watching the silent interaction between them. "Won it how?"

Before Max could answer, Jason waggled his head in dismay. "I thought you loved that car."

"I love this woman more."

Rachel's breath stopped. Without his arm propelling her forward, her feet would have stopped as well. Instead, she kept going, stumbling over the transition from hardwood floor to area rug. Max's strong arm supported her. His steady calm soothed her flustered emotions.

She regained her balance, physically and spiritually, and stared up at him in awe. "You do?"

"Of course he does," Jason grumbled. "He's giving up the find of a lifetime because of you."

Max shot his best friend a sour look. Jason retaliated with a disgruntled glare of his own. The undercurrents in the room darted around her like agitated birds. Rachel wasn't sure what was going on, but she sensed she was at the heart of it.

"You don't have to give up your car for me."

Max took her hands in his and deposited kisses in both palms. "I'm not giving it up for you. I'm giving it up because I lost a bet."

"What sort of bet?"

"I bet him he'd marry whoever your agency placed as his assistant," Jason explained.

The absurdity of it made her laugh. "You were serious

about all that?" she asked him. "I thought for sure you'd made it all up as payback for what I did to you five years ago."

"No," Jason said. "We were completely serious. Do you have any idea how many men have married the assistants you've placed with them?"

"You're both insane."

"Nine." Jason crossed to a table with three crystal decanters and poured himself a shot out of one. When he gestured toward them with the bottle, both she and Max shook their heads. "Nine perfectly happy bachelors have fallen in love. Including my father. His brother. And now my best friend. All because of you."

"I wasn't perfectly happy," Max insisted.

Rachel turned on Jason. "You're behind his idiotic idea that I run a matchmaking service? You can't seriously think I have anything to do with those couples falling in love."

Jason scowled at her. "You match executives and assistants. A lot of them get married."

His claim was so preposterous she didn't know how to refute it. "That's crazy."

"Is it?" Jason gestured behind her.

Rachel turned. To her astonishment, Max dropped to one knee and produced a ring from his pocket. "Rachel Lansing. Will you marry me?"

Rachel covered her gasp with both hands as she stared from the man she adored to the ring he held out to her. The large diamond sparkled, hypnotizing her. Her thoughts began to circle. Max wanted to marry her. He loved her. They would live together in his big house and have lots of babies. At least she hoped they would. She had no idea of his views on children. Or any of a hundred things that couples heading toward marriage talked about.

"Answer him," Jason bellowed, his impatience spilling over.

"Yes."

Grinning, Max slid the ring on her finger. He got to his feet and cupped her face, drinking from her lips, long and deep.

By the time they came up for air, Jason had collapsed onto the couch and was staring at the empty glass in his hand.

"What's wrong with him?" Rachel whispered, nudging her head toward Jason. "He looks like he's lost his best friend."

Max's grin was pure mischief. "He's sad because he's a miserable, lonely bachelor."

"Does he need an executive assistant?"

Jason came off the couch with a roar. "Don't you dare."

Laughing, Max and Rachel retreated from the house. As Max drove her car back to his place, Rachel leaned her head against the seat rest and admired the ring on her hand. "Do you think there's anything to Jason's claim of matchmaking?"

"No." His scoffing tone was at odds with his uncertain frown. "But maybe in the future all the assistants you place at Case Consolidated Holdings should be old and married."

Rachel laughed. "I think that can be arranged."

* * * * *

PASSION

Harlequin® Desire

COMING NEXT MONTH
AVAILABLE MAY 8, 2012

#2155 UNDONE BY HER TENDER TOUCH
Pregnancy & Passion
Maya Banks
When one night with magnate Cam Hollingsworth results in pregnancy, no-strings-attached turns into a tangled web for caterer Pippa Laingley.

#2156 ONE DANCE WITH THE SHEIKH
Dynasties: The Kincaids
Tessa Radley

#2157 THE TIES THAT BIND
Billionaires and Babies
Emilie Rose

#2158 AN INTIMATE BARGAIN
Colorado Cattle Barons
Barbara Dunlop

#2159 RELENTLESS PURSUIT
Lone Star Legacy
Sara Orwig

#2160 READY FOR HER CLOSE-UP
Matchmakers, Inc.
Katherine Garbera

REQUEST YOUR FREE BOOKS!

2 FREE NOVELS PLUS 2 FREE GIFTS!

Harlequin® Desire

ALWAYS POWERFUL, PASSIONATE AND PROVOCATIVE

YES! Please send me 2 FREE Harlequin Desire® novels and my 2 FREE gifts (gifts are worth about $10). After receiving them, if I don't wish to receive any more books, I can return the shipping statement marked "cancel." If I don't cancel, I will receive 6 brand-new novels every month and be billed just $4.30 per book in the U.S. or $4.99 per book in Canada. That's a saving of at least 14% off the cover price! It's quite a bargain! Shipping and handling is just 50¢ per book in the U.S. and 75¢ per book in Canada.* I understand that accepting the 2 free books and gifts places me under no obligation to buy anything. I can always return a shipment and cancel at any time. Even if I never buy another book, the two free books and gifts are mine to keep forever.

225/326 HDN FEF3

Name _____ (PLEASE PRINT)

Address _____ Apt. #

City _____ State/Prov. _____ Zip/Postal Code

Signature (if under 18, a parent or guardian must sign)

Mail to the **Reader Service:**
IN U.S.A.: P.O. Box 1867, Buffalo, NY 14240-1867
IN CANADA: P.O. Box 609, Fort Erie, Ontario L2A 5X3

Not valid for current subscribers to Harlequin Desire books.

Want to try two free books from another line?
Call 1-800-873-8635 or visit www.ReaderService.com.

* Terms and prices subject to change without notice. Prices do not include applicable taxes. Sales tax applicable in N.Y. Canadian residents will be charged applicable taxes. Offer not valid in Quebec. This offer is limited to one order per household. All orders subject to credit approval. Credit or debit balances in a customer's account(s) may be offset by any other outstanding balance owed by or to the customer. Please allow 4 to 6 weeks for delivery. Offer available while quantities last.

Your Privacy—The Reader Service is committed to protecting your privacy. Our Privacy Policy is available online at www.ReaderService.com or upon request from the Reader Service.

We make a portion of our mailing list available to reputable third parties that offer products we believe may interest you. If you prefer that we not exchange your name with third parties, or if you wish to clarify or modify your communication preferences, please visit us at www.ReaderService.com/consumerchoice or write to us at Reader Service Preference Service, P.O. Box 9062, Buffalo, NY 14269. Include your complete name and address.

HDES11B

New York Times *and* USA TODAY *bestselling author*
Maya Banks presents book four in her miniseries
PREGNANCY & PASSION

UNDONE BY HER TENDER TOUCH

Available May 2012 from Harlequin® Desire!

"**W**ould you like some help?"

Pippa whirled around, still holding the bottle of champagne, and darn near tossed the contents onto the floor.

"Help?"

Cam nodded slowly. "Assistance? You look as though you could use it. How on earth did you think you'd manage to cater this event on your own?"

Pippa was horrified by his offer and then, as she processed the rest of his statement, she was irritated as hell.

"I'd hate for you to sully those pretty hands," she snapped. "And for your information, I've got this under control. The help didn't show. Not my fault. The food is impeccable, if I do say so myself. I just need to deliver it to the guests."

"I believe I just offered my assistance and you insulted me," Cam said dryly.

Her eyebrows drew together. Oh, why did the man have to be so damn delicious-looking? And why could she never perform the simplest functions around him?

"You're Ashley's guest," Pippa said firmly. "Not to mention you're used to being served, not serving others."

"How do you know what I'm used to?" he asked mildly.

She had absolutely nothing to say to that and watched in bewilderment as he hefted the tray up and walked out of the kitchen.

She sagged against the sink, her pulse racing hard enough

to make her dizzy.

Cameron Hollingsworth was gorgeous, unpolished in a rough and totally sexy way, arrogant and so wrong for her. But there was something about the man that just did it for her.

She sighed. He was a luscious specimen of a male and he couldn't be any less interested in her.

Even so, she was itching to shake his world up a little.

Realizing she was spending far too much time mooning over Cameron, she grabbed another tray, took a deep breath to compose herself and then headed toward the living room.

And Cameron Hollingsworth.

Will Pippa shake up Cameron's world?
Find out in Maya Banks's passionate new novel

UNDONE BY HER TENDER TOUCH

Available May 2012 from Harlequin® Desire!

Royalty has never been so scandalous!

When Crown Prince Alessandro of Santina proposes
to paparazzi favorite Allegra Jackson it promises
to be *the* social event of the decade!

Harlequin Presents® invites you to step into the decadent
playground of the world's rich and famous and rub shoulders
with royalty, sheikhs and glamorous socialites.

**Collect all 8 passionate tales written by *USA TODAY*
bestselling authors, beginning May 2012!**